LOVE'S SIGHT

LOVE'S MAGIC BOOK 7

BETTY MCLAIN

This book is dedicated to all who have overcome their hardships to locate and hold onto true love.

CHAPTER 1

*M*arissa Embers knocked on the door of Laura Sands' bedroom. When she did not get an answer, she opened the door and peeked inside. She saw Laura, with earphones in her ears, listening to music and sitting in a chair by the window.

Marissa entered the room and tapped Laura on the shoulder. Laura jumped and turned toward Marissa. "Who's there?" she asked.

"It's just me," said Marissa. "I didn't mean to scare you. I just wanted to let you know I was here."

Laura's sightless eyes stared at where Marissa's voice was coming from. Laura smiled. Marissa had been her best friend for a long time. She might fuss at others for bothering her, but never Marissa. "What are you doing here? Don't you have to work?" asked Laura.

"Today is my day off," said Marissa. "I came by to see if you would go to Danny's with me," said Marissa.

Laura started shaking her head. She had been very reclusive since she lost her sight in a tumble down the stairs a month before. She tripped over a toy on a stair step and tumbled all the way down the stairs, hitting her head on the banister at the bottom. Unconscious, she was rushed to the hospital. After she regained consciousness, she was unable to see. Dr. Holly Smith, her specialist, said she might get her sight back. They would just have to wait and see. Laura was losing hope. She was beginning to think she was going to be permanently blind.

"Please, say you will go with me. I want to look in the mirror, but I don't want to go by myself," begged Marissa. "You can hold onto my arm. No one will notice a thing."

"Why do you keep looking in the mirror? You have not seen anyone, yet," said Laura.

"I can't give up. I know my true love is out there," said Marissa.

"Okay, I would not do this for anyone else. Do my clothes and hair look alright?" asked Laura.

"Your clothes are fine. Sit still, and I'll fix your hair," said Marissa. She took the hair brush and proceeded to style Laura's hair.

"You know," said Laura. "You need to go to beautician school. You are really good at fixing hair."

"I am thinking about it," said Marissa. "As soon as I save enough money, I will go." Giving Laura's hair one last pat, she handed Laura her cane and, taking her arm, led her out of her room, down the stairs, and out to her car.

Marissa drove to Danny's Bar and Grill. It was a popular place to eat in town and had been even more popular since Marsha Dane brought a magic mirror to Sharpville. It was past dinner time, so the place was not crowded. There were only a few stragglers around. They were leaving as Laura and Marissa entered.

Marissa led Laura over to the table with the mirror and helped her be seated in the chair in front of it.

"I have to run to the restroom. You sit here and hold my place for me. I'll be right back," promised Marissa.

Laura did not say anything. Silently willing Marissa to hurry, she turned toward the mirror as if she could see it. She had the strangest feeling someone was watching her.

In Kansas City, Joseph Hillard was leaving the men's room on the way back to work, when he glanced in the mirror and saw a girl looking back at him. He looked around, but no-one was there. He looked back at the mirror, and she was still sitting there, looking straight at him. He looked at her background. It was familiar, but he couldn't place it. The girl started to fade, and he was looking at his own reflection again. He sighed. He did not have time for this. He had work to do. The type was not going to set itself. He had a newspaper to get printed. His ghost girl would just have to haunt someone else. Joseph went back to work, and even though he tried, he could not quite get the ghost girl out of his mind. She kept intruding into his thoughts.

Marissa returned and sat down in a chair next to Laura. She looked in the mirror, but she only saw herself and Laura. She sighed.

"Is anyone else here besides us?" asked Laura.

Marissa looked around. There was no one there. She knew the workers were in the kitchen cleaning up from lunch. "No, everyone is in the kitchen, why?" she asked.

"I got the strangest feeling. It felt like someone was staring at me," said Laura with a shiver.

"Maybe the waitress came in to clear a table," said Marissa.

"Maybe," responded Laura. "I did not hear any dishes being loaded. It was very quiet."

Marissa looked around again. She looked out the window.

"Maybe someone was passing the window outside," she suggested.

"Maybe," agreed Laura.

"Do you want to get something to eat while we are here?" asked Marissa.

"No, I am not hungry," said Laura. She was still nervous about eating in public.

Brian Dane came in from the back. He looked surprised to see Laura sitting at the table with the mirror. He headed over to say hello.

"Hello, Laura, Marissa, how are you ladies doing today?" he asked.

"We are okay, Brian," said Marissa.

"Could I get you something to eat or drink?" he asked.

Laura shook her head.

"I am glad to see you out, Laura. I know Mary and Gary have been worried about you. Your parents were very upset after your accident," he said.

"I know, but there is nothing to do but wait. The doctor says I might get my sight back," said Laura.

"It is always possible," agreed Brian. "I had lost my memory for years, and the doctor told me I might get it back. I had given up hope until my wife found me. It came back in a rush. There is always hope. Don't give up."

"I won't," said Laura, with a smile. "I just have to use some of my very non-existent patience."

Brian laughed along with her and Marissa. "Let me get you

both a glass of iced tea," suggested Brian. "There is no one else here. You can practice drinking in public. It is on the house"

"Okay," agreed Laura.

Brian left to get two iced teas and bring them over to them. "Enjoy, ladies. Laura, don't be a stranger. Cindy misses seeing you." Brian returned to the back. Laura and Marissa settled back to enjoy their iced tea.

Cindy Rhea, his and Marsha's four-year-old daughter, and the light of their lives, was named after their friend from Rolling Fork, who helped them get back together by lending Marsha the magic mirror. The mirror showed Brian alive, when Marsha had been told he was dead. They would forever be grateful to Cindy and the magic mirror.

When Cindy told Marsha to keep the mirror, Marsha wanted to display it in Danny's Bar and Grill. She wanted to give other ladies a chance to find their true loves. It was a main attraction for ladies in Sharpville and the surrounding towns. Word of it spread. A lot of ladies made special trips just to gaze in the mirror. Some saw their guys in the mirror. Some did not, but they kept hoping and looking.

While they were enjoying their tea, Marsha came in. She had Cindy with her. When Marsha saw Laura and Marissa sitting at the table, she came over. "Laura, I am so glad to see you out and about. I just saw your mom at the nursery, when I picked up Cindy," said Marsha. She picked Cindy up from the Little Tots nursery when she finished her shift at work at the police department. "Hello, Marissa, I'm glad to see you managed to get Laura to visit us."

"Hello, Mrs. Dane," said Marissa.

"Hello, Mrs. Dane, I'm glad to get a chance to say hello to Cindy," said Laura.

Cindy was leaning against Laura's leg, waiting to be noticed.

"Hi, Cindy." said Laura. She rubbed her hand over the top of the little girl's head and leaned down to give her a hug.

"Hi," said Cindy, shyly.

Brian came into the room, and Cindy abandoned Laura and ran to her dad.

"Daddy!" she squealed and threw herself into his arms to be picked up. Brian obliged her and swung her up in his arms.

Marsha followed her over and raised her face for a kiss. Brian was happy to kiss both of his girls, but he lingered a bit with Marsha.

"We were on our way home, but Little Miss wanted to stop and see Daddy first," said Marsha. "I'm always happy for an excuse to stop and see Daddy." Marsha raised her face for another kiss. Brian smiled down at her while kissing her.

Marsha came back over to Laura and Marissa's table. She smiled at Marissa.

"Have you had any luck with the mirror?" she asked.

Marissa shook her head. "No," she said on a sigh.

Well, don't give up. It is possible your true love is not near a mirror. He may be working in a job without reflective surfaces around. You can only see him if he can be reflected back at you," she smiled at Marissa.

Marissa looked thoughtful. "Maybe I need to look in the mirror at night," she said.

Marsha shrugged. "It could not hurt to try," she agreed.

"It was nice to bump into you both, but I need to get my Little Miss home and start supper," said Marsha. She reached for Cindy and gave Brian another kiss and, with a wave, left for home.

Brian came over to the table to see if they needed anything. When they said they were fine, he returned to the back room.

"We need to go," said Laura. "I'm not staying for hours so you can check out the mirror at night."

Marissa laughed. "I know," she said. "I will try some other time."

She helped Laura out to the car. After she helped buckle her in, she took her back to her house. Marissa went in with her to make sure she made it up the stairs to her room safely.

Laura's brother, Mac, followed them upstairs. Mac was short for Macland. It was their mother's maiden name and a trial for Mac at times. He had endured teasing about his name on numerous occasions.

Marissa helped Laura into her room and said goodbye. She promised she would be back soon.

After she left, Mac came into Laura's room. "Could I talk to you for a minute?" he asked Laura.

"Sure, Mac, what is it?" asked Laura.

"I just wanted to say I'm sorry about you getting hurt. If I had not dropped my toy on the step, and forgot to come back for it, you would not have fallen," he said tearfully.

"It was not your fault, Mac," said Laura, standing and hugging her young brother. "I was in a hurry and was not paying attention. It was an accident. No one is to blame. Anyway, the doctor said I could get my sight back. We just have to wait and see. Quit worrying about me and go get your homework done. If you need any help, come to me. Even if I can't see, you can read it to me, and I can help."

"Thanks, Laura, I have finished my homework tonight, but I will remember for tomorrow," said Mac. He left sounding like a weight had been lifted from his shoulders.

When Mac left, Laura sighed. Whether she got her sight back or not, she could not have her little brother torturing himself with guilt. It had been an accident. She tripped. She did not know if the toy was at fault or not. Either way, it was not Mac's fault. She should have been more careful.

"Hi," said Tilly, nervously. "Can I come in?" Tilly did not

seem to know how to act around Laura since her loss of eyesight.

"Sure," said Laura. Tilly, short for Matilda, was Laura's sister. "How is school going?" asked Laura. Tilly was seventeen, so this was her senior year in school.

"It's going good. I aced my last tests. I am glad I am in advanced classes. It will help bring up my GPA," said Tilly.

"Congratulations, you have done great in advanced classes. Has Stephan asked you to be his date for the prom?" asked Laura.

"Yes, he asked me today. I was wondering if I could borrow your prom dress. We are the same size, and you only wore it once. It would save Mom and Dad having to buy another dress, and I have always loved your dress," said Tilly pleadingly.

"Absolutely," laughed Laura. "I will be glad to see my dress get used again." She stopped abruptly when she realized what she said. Tilly shifted uncomfortably.

"It is just a saying," said Laura. "My dress is in my closet. It is in a bag to protect it. Go ahead and take it with you, now. It may need cleaning."

"Thanks, Laura," said Tilly, giving Laura a hug.

"You are very welcome," said Laura.

Tilly headed for Laura's closet and came out with the dress in a clothing bag. "I'll take this down to Mom," she said excitedly as she left.

Laura sat back smiling. She was glad her sister's high school crush had finally got up the nerve to ask her to the prom. Tilly had been dreaming about him for a while. They were both too shy to do anything about it. It ought to be an interesting evening. Laura laughed.

She thought back to her crush in school. She had been only in seventh grade when she noticed him. He did not even know she existed. He was three years ahead of her in school. She never talked to him. She just drooled over him from afar. The only one who knew how she had felt was Marissa. Joe disappeared from Sharpville when he graduated. As far as she knew, he had not been back. None of the other boys in school or later had ever measured up to Joe. He set a very high standard in her heart.

Laura sighed and reached for ear plugs. She needed to get her mind off Joe. She did not know why he was on her mind all of a sudden. Maybe it was thinking about Tilly's date with Stephan. It was time to move on. Joe was long gone.

CHAPTER 2

The next three weeks were busy. Laura made two more visits to the doctor. There had been no change in her eyesight. She made another visit to Danny's Bar and Grill with Marissa. Marissa was hoping the mirror would show her guy to her. She had come away disappointed. Everyone urged her to be patient. It was hard to keep her spirits up after so many tries without results.

Tilly was busy with finals and very excited about the upcoming prom. Mac asked Laura for help on his homework and seemed to understand it after she explained it to him. He told her she would make a good teacher. He said she made it much easier to understand. He was not confused after she helped.

Laura was glad she could help her brother, but unless her eyesight returned there was no way she could think about getting training as a teacher. Even if she had training, it would be next to impossible to get a position teaching. Laura was beginning to worry about her life from now on. She knew her parents did not have the money to keep paying for all of her expensive medical care. Their insurance only went so far. There was a large deductible, and they were struggling. Her dad was a policeman and her mom was working at Little Tots nursery. The police department helped out. They had a fund to help the families of policemen in need. But the bills kept coming in, and the income did not stretch far enough.

Laura was glad she could furnish Tilly with a prom dress. It would be one less expense. Her folks told her not to worry, they would manage, but Laura overheard her dad talking about taking a night job as a security guard.

Laura decided enough was enough. If she was going to be stuck like this, she had to be able to contribute in some way. While everyone was gone, she decided to go downstairs and learn her way around.

Laura got her cane and walked out of her room. She knew there would be no one here for several hours. She carefully made her way down the stairs and, counting steps and using her cane, learned where everything was located, in the living room. She then counted her way down the hall into the dining room. She slowly made her way around the table several times. It was strange. You think everything is clear in your head, but it all seemed different when you couldn't see it.

Laura made her way into the kitchen. She went around the cabinets. Using her cane and counting, she walked around the kitchen. She located the stove, the sink, and the refrigerator. When she was at the sink, she discovered the crock pot was on the cabinet. It felt warm to the touch. Her mom must have left tonight's meal cooking. It smelled good, she thought.

Laura made her way to the laundry room. She stood in the door, but didn't go in. Next, she found the back door. She carefully unlocked the door and went out onto the porch. She made her way over to a chair and sat down.

The breeze felt good. It felt good to be out of her room.

Laura leaned back and closed her eyes. She sat there for several minutes, just enjoying the cool air on her face. When she sighed and sat up, she opened her eyes. She was startled to see light, instead of the dark she was used to seeing. She blinked her eyes and the light was gone. It was dark again. Laura shook her head. She could not have imagined it. She did not know what it meant, but she had seen light. She had hope again, after months of despair.

Laura got out of the chair and carefully, with the help of her cane, made her way inside. She locked the door and counted her way out of the kitchen and down the hall. She counted the steps up the stairs and to her room. She walked around, but she was too excited to sit still. She decided to go back downstairs.

Laura carefully made her way back down stairs. She went over and sat on the sofa. She felt on the table, next to the sofa, and found the remote for the television. Pointing it in the direction of the television, she clicked the on button. It came on, and she changed channels until she found a news channel. It was time to rejoin the world. It did not stop just because she was blind.

Laura had been listening, for about an hour, when the doorbell rang. Laura took her cane and made her way over to answer the door.

"Who is it?" she called through the door.

"It's me, Marissa." Laura opened the door and Marissa came in and hugged her. "I am so glad to see you up and about," she said.

"I thought it was time to stop feeling sorry for myself," said Laura.

"You needed some recovery time," said Marissa.

"Today must be your day off," said Laura.

"Yes, it is. I need to go shopping. My shoes have had it. I

also want to take another look in the mirror," Marissa declared, as if daring Laura to disagree with her. Laura just laughed. She was feeling too good after seeing the light to argue with Marissa about the mirror. "You will come with me, won't you?" asked Marissa.

"Sure," said Laura. "Will you run upstairs and get my purse and phone?"

Marissa looked at Laura. She was surprised at her ready agreement, but she was not giving her time to change her mind. Marissa hurried upstairs to get Laura's phone and purse.

"I'm going to have to get a clip to wear my phone. I need to have it on me in case of emergencies," said Laura taking the requested items and putting the phone in her pocket.

"Where are we going first?" Laura asked when they were on their way.

"I want to check the mirror first. It is almost lunch time. Anyone working may be on lunch break," said Marissa.

"Good idea," agreed Laura.

When they sat at the table with the mirror on it, they ordered a burger and iced tea. After their order came, Marissa stared into the mirror. She seemed to be trying to force it to work. All of a sudden, she saw the reflection of a man. It looked like he was reflected in water. His hair and face were wet. He looked like he ducked his head in the water. He had his eyes closed as he shook his head and grabbed a towel to dry with. He opened his eyes, but he wasn't looking at her. Marissa had no idea who he was, although he looked familiar. Something about him teased the back of her mind. The mirror started to fade. He looked straight at her just as the image went away.

Jed Hillard shook his head. Now he was seeing things. He needed to take a day off. The work was getting to him. He could leave Les and Dan in charge of the dairy and take a couple of days off. He did not have time to be haunted. Although, from what he saw of her, she was a nice-looking ghost. He only got one look at her before she was gone.

Marissa sat back with a sigh.

"What is it?" asked Laura. "Did you see someone?"

"Yes, I did," said Marissa.

"You did?" said Laura with a gasp. "Who was he?"

"I don't know. He looked familiar, but I just can't place from where."

"Did he see you?" asked Laura.

"Yes, just for a few seconds. I'm sure he thought he was hallucinating. He looked so startled," laughed Marissa.

"Well, now you have seen him, you just have to keep your eyes open and hope you see him again," said Laura.

"Yes," agreed Marissa. "That is all I can do."

Marissa looked at their empty plates and laughed. "Let's go shoe shopping," she said. She grabbed the ticket and helped Laura to stand. They headed for the front desk. Marissa paid the bill and they went outside.

"I want to pay my share," said Laura, when they were in the car. She handed her purse to Marissa and told her to take out the money for her lunch.

Marissa refused. "I brought you along, so I could look in the mirror. I didn't want to sit there by myself. The lunch is my treat."

"Thanks," said Laura after she thought about what Marissa said.

Marissa found just the shoes to suit her at a small shoe store. "I always go to Shoe Gold," she said. "Since I found them, I have had no trouble finding just the right shoes."

"I know," agreed Laura. "I was with you when you discovered them. Anyone would have thought you had struck it rich."

"The perfect shoe makes me feel like I am rich," declared Marissa. She and Laura laughed together.

Marissa wanted to stop back by Danny's Bar and Grill before she drove Laura home. She said she wanted to celebrate finding the perfect shoes, but Laura knew it was to take another look in the mirror.

There were a few customers there, but the evening crowd had not started arriving, so no-one was at the table with the mirror. Marissa led Laura to the mirror table and left to wash her hands and pick up tea for them. Laura sat facing the mirror.

Joe was getting ready to leave his job. He was getting off early to take a test in his class at the university. He walked by a mirror in the hall but stopped abruptly when he saw the same woman he had seen before in the bathroom. She looked like she was in the same place as before.

"Who are you?" he asked.

Laura started. "Who's there?" she asked.

"I asked you first," said Joe. "Are you a ghost?"

A ghost? What a strange thing for someone to say ... unless he was seeing her through the mirror. "No, I'm not a ghost. I can't see you, though. I am blind," said Laura. "So, who are you?"

"I'm sorry," said Joe. "My name is Joseph. Who are you?"

"My name is Laura. You can see me because I am sitting in front of a magic mirror. It's supposed to show girls their true love. It doesn't do any good for it to show me. I can't see anyone," she finished abruptly, feeling slightly bitter.

"I'm sorry. How long have you been blind?" Joe asked.

Laura was surprised at his question. He completely ignored that they were talking through a magic true love mirror and asked about her blindness. "Not long. I fell down a flight of stairs and hit my head. I have been blind since I awakened," Laura explained.

"Will you get your sight back," said Joe.

"The doctor said it's possible, but I sure hate being a burden on everyone," Laura said sadly.

"I'm sure your family is glad you are okay. They won't feel like you are a burden," said Joe.

"I suppose so. They have all been very supportive," agreed Laura.

Joe looked at his watch. "I have to go. I'm taking night classes and I have a test tonight. Maybe I'll see you again," said Joe.

"Maybe, good luck on your test," said Laura.

"Thank you. Goodbye," said Joe. The mirror faded and Joe, with a sigh, headed to class.

Marissa came back with their drinks. Laura did not tell her about her conversation with the mysterious Joseph. He reminded her of her high school crush on Joe Hillard. Laura shook her head. She did not know why she had Joe Hillard on her mind so much lately. He had been gone a long time.

Joe hurried into his class and took his seat. His professor gave him a look, but did not say anything. Joe tried to concentrate on his test, but it was hard. His mind kept going back to the girl in the mirror. She was nice looking. He felt like he should know her. Something about her teased the back of his mind. He shook his head and tried to concentrate on his test. He was in the final lap of his education. He had almost finished his degree in journalism. After leaving the farm and refusing to have anything to do with the dairy, he was determined not to fail. He had to prove to Jed he could make it on his own, without help.

The last fight he had with Jed, when Jed accused him of messing around with his fiancée, Sharon, was always on his mind. Jed refused to believe him about being innocent. He threw a punch at him. Well, he had to leave. He could not stay where he was not believed.

The test was finally over and Joe turned in his paper and hoped for the best. His mind had been on everything but the test. If he passed, it would be a miracle.

Back at Danny's Bar and Grill, Marissa was back at the table. She kept staring at the mirror but not seeing her guy. She was about to give up when the mirror flashed on. The man she saw before was sitting at a very familiar bar. He was in front of a large mirror. The mirror was in front of the bar at Danny's Bar and Grill.

Marissa looked up, startled. She looked toward the bar, sure enough, her guy was sitting there, joking with Brian and Danny. They were not looking at the mirror. Her guy looked up and stared straight at Marissa. Jed shook his head. Now, his ghost woman was following him around. He did not say anything. He did not want his friends to think he was crazy. He just kept staring at the mirror.

Marissa smiled at him. He did not smile back. While he was looking Marissa over, she had been checking him out. He was dressed nicely, but a little more rugged then she was used to. The mirror took its time to fade out. Marissa looked over at the bar and saw her guy shake his head. He seemed to be denying what he had seen.

Well, she could not have that. "I'll be right back," she told Laura. "I'm going to get a refill. Do you want anything?"

"No, thank you," said Laura.

Marissa walked slowly over to the bar. Her heart was pounding, but she tried to act sure of herself. She walked up beside her guy and spoke to Brian.

"Could I get a refill please?' she asked handing him her glass.

"Sure, Marissa, does Laura need anything?" asked Brian.

"No, she is fine, thanks," said Marissa.

Her guy turned sharply and stared at her. She smiled at him and Brian and, taking her glass, turned and walked away.

"Who was she?" asked Jed of Brian and Danny after Marissa returned to her seat.

"Her name is Marissa Embers. She works at the drug store. She is Laura's best friend and has been encouraging her to get out more since the accident left her blind," said Brian.

"Her friend is blind?" asked Jed.

"Yes, she fell down a flight of stairs a couple of months ago. She hit her head and has not been able to see since then," said Brian.

"Is she going to get better?" asked Jed.

"We don't know yet," responded Brian.

Danny had been watching Jed. He saw how Jed was asking questions about Laura, but he never took his eyes off Marissa. Danny turned away to hide a smile.

Marissa returned to the table and sat down. "My guy is here," she told Laura quietly.

Laura looked up startled. "He's here?" she asked.

"Yes," replied Marissa. "He is over at the bar talking to Brian and Danny."

"Did you talk to him?" asked Laura.

"No, I just wanted to make sure he saw me. I wanted him to know I was not a ghost," she replied. "Are you ready to go?'

Laura got up and prepared to leave.

"You are going to leave, now?" she asked.

"Yes," agreed Marissa. "My guy is going to have to do the chasing. I am not chasing him. He is going to have to want me in his life as much as I want him."

Marissa never looked at the bar as she and Laura made their way outside, but she was sure the guy at the bar was watching her and Laura all the way out of the door. She smiled to herself. This could be fun and interesting.

Jed watched the girls make their way to the door. When they were gone, he sighed and turned his attention back to Brian and Danny. Brian and Danny had noticed his attention following the girls, but they did not say anything.

"How are things going at the dairy?" asked Brian.

"We are doing good. I am thinking about taking some time off. I haven't had a vacation in a long time," remarked Jed.

"Have you had any news about Joe?" asked Danny.

"No, I have not had any news from him since he left. I should have listened to him, but I was so caught up in Sharon's lies, I thought I knew it all," remarked Jed shaking his head.

Danny and Brian knew all about his confrontation with Joe and its outcome. They also knew about Jed finding Sharon making out with one of his former dairy workers.

Jed had been on his way to town and remembered that he had left his shopping list in his office. He went back to get it and found Sharon and Smiley doing some heavy petting in his office. He stood, stunned, in the doorway watching until they noticed him. Sharon had tried to say she was fighting off an attack, but he had seen enough to know it was not true. He had believed her over Joe, when she had claimed the same thing.

Joe said Sharon was making a pass at him. Jed had not believed him. He punched Joe. When Joe got up, he shook his head. He did not say anything to Jed. He just looked at him sadly and went in the house. It was the last time he saw his brother. When he came in after milking, Joe had packed his clothes and left. He told his dad and mom he could not stay on the dairy farm with Jed and Sharon.

When Jed had found Sharon with Smiley, he broke their engagement and told her to get her things and leave. He told her if she was not gone by the time he came back from town, he would call the sheriff and have her escorted off his land. A very angry Sharon was gone by the time Jed returned. Jed had told Brian and Danny the whole story while drinking at the bar. He noticed as he told them, neither had looked surprised. Sharon must have made herself a reputation in town. He was well rid of her. He was not in any hurry to get tangled up with another woman.

CHAPTER 3

*E*ven though Jed was not looking to get involved with another woman, he could not get Marissa Embers off his mind. He found himself looking in every mirror he passed. When he was around any reflective surface, she would pop into his mind. He tried to ignore his thoughts of her, but there was something about her he could not forget.

He was grumpy around his workers and short with his parents, when he went in for lunch. He apologized to his mom and dad. They looked at him strangely but accepted his apology. He did not apologize to his workers. He was planning on taking some time off. Maybe his grumpiness would help them understand why he needed a break.

Meanwhile Joe was having similar problems. He was thinking a lot about Laura. After he left the farm, he had written to his mom, so she would not worry about him. He made her promise not to tell Jed where he was and what he was doing. He called her regularly to check on her and his dad and to let her know he was doing okay. His dad was retired, due to a stroke. He had to be on a strict diet and was paralyzed on one side. His Mom had a live-in helper to help take care of him. He did not want to add to their worries. If he had stayed on the farm, there would have been more trouble between him and Jed. It would have been stressful for his parents.

When he first arrived in Kansas City, he took a job on a construction site to earn enough money to live on until he could do better. He had saved his money from a part time job in high school. He had enough to rent a room and eat until he could earn a paycheck. After working on the construction job for a couple of months, he bumped into a reporter from the newspaper at a local cafe. The reporter told him there was a job opening at the newspaper for a typesetter. It just so happened, Joe had worked as a typesetter at Sharpville's newspaper during summer vacation, between ninth and tenth grade in high school. He applied and got the job.

He decided to stay in the room he had rented and to save money so he could take university classes at night. He began working toward his degree in journalism. It had been his dream and main focus until Laura popped up in his mirror and started haunting him.

Joe could not stop thinking about her. She was a beautiful girl, and to be stuck without her sight must have been devastating for her. He wondered how the mirror she was sitting in front of could show them to each other. He had never heard of such a thing happening.

Laura said something about the mirror showing a person their true love. Was it possible, Laura was his true love? He did not even know her or where she lived. She could not see him. How did she know how she would feel about him? He did not know how he felt about her. He just knew everything about her kept going around in his head.

Joe took his shower and tried to lie down and get some sleep. He had to be up early to get to work. He was going in early to make up for taking off early today for his test. He lay there for a while, thinking about Laura, before finally drifting off. He felt like he had just got to sleep when his alarm said it was time to get up. He forced himself to get up and prepare for another day, working at a job he really liked doing.

Laura was thinking about Joe, also. Her dreams had been full of Joe Hillard. She kept reliving her conversations with Joe in the mirror, but somehow Joe Hillard face seemed to be in her dream. The two were connected, maybe because she had not seen the Joe in the mirror and had no face to match with the voice. She woke up determined to go to the mirror again. Laura used the voice commands on her phone to call Marissa. She wanted to know when she was going to look in the mirror again.

"Hello," said Marissa.

"Hi, do you have any updates on your guy?" asked Laura.

"No, I did not expect anything this soon," said Marissa. "I am going by to check the mirror at lunch time. I would not want him to forget me. I want to be very much on his mind."

Laura laughed. Leave it to Marissa to make love a challenge. "Are you going to come by and pick me up?" she asked.

"Sure, I'll be by. I need all the support I can get. I have to have an excuse for sitting in front of the mirror," Marissa laughed.

"I'll be ready. Have a good day at work," replied Laura.

"Yeah, right, I'm so excited about finding my guy, I will float through the work," said Marissa. "Bye."

Laura hung up the phone with a smile on her face. Maybe she would get to talk to Joe again.

When Marissa came by at lunchtime, Laura went out as soon as she heard the car stop. Marissa opened the door and helped her get settled. "I should have found my guy earlier. If it would have got you up and out of the house," she said with a laugh.

"I am very happy for you," replied Laura with a smile

Marissa glanced at her curiously, but shrugged her shoulders and headed for Danny's.

There was someone sitting at the table with the mirror when they entered Danny's. They sat at the bar to wait for the girl to leave. Brian came over and asked for their order.

"Two burgers with fries and two iced teas," replied Marissa. Laura smiled at Marissa's high-handed ordering for her without asking.

When Brian came back over from turning in their order, Marissa caught his attention.

"When we were here last, you and Danny were talking to someone at the bar. I thought I recognized him, but I can't place him," said Marissa.

Brian thought for a minute.

"Oh, we were talking to Jed Hillard," he said.

"Jed Hillard, you mean Joe Hillard's brother?" asked Marissa.

"Yes, do you know Joe?" he asked.

"We went to school with him. He was three years ahead of us in school, so we didn't really know him," replied Marissa, with a quick look at Laura. The girl left the mirror table, so Marissa grabbed Laura's hand to help her to the table. "We need to get our table before someone else does," said Marissa.

"Okay I'll send out your food when it is ready," agreed Brian.

Brian shook his head. If Marissa had seen Jed in the mirror, Jed may as well quit running and give in gracefully. He was no match for a determined Marissa. Brian laughed. There was no chance for boredom in this town. There was always something to keep life interesting. Marsha had informed him last night, she was going to be on duty at this year's prom, and he was going to be her escort. At least he would get to dance with his wife. Grinning, Brian went back to work.

Marissa and Laura sat at the table and stared at the mirror. Nothing was happening. The waitress brought their food over and they started eating. Marissa was keeping an eye on the mirror. Suddenly the mirror showed Jed as he was entering his house. It looked like the mirror was in the entrance hall.

"Jed," she whispered.

Jed's head went up and he stared at the mirror.

Marissa smiled at him.

"Why are you haunting me?" he asked.

Marissa's smile faded. "I'm not haunting you," she said.

"Why do you keep popping up?" he asked.

"I have no control over what the mirror does. It has a mind of its own. I just look in it. Why are you so angry? I am not doing anything but looking in the magic mirror. You do not have to look back," declared Marissa.

"It is a little hard to ignore a woman's face in your mirror. Especially one like yours," said Jed.

"I like your face, too," said Marissa smiling. Jed shook his head and smiled. She was determined to put a good spin on things. "I knew you could smile," said Marissa with satisfaction. The mirror faded leaving both of them dissatisfied with the way things had ended.

Laura had been sitting quietly, listening to Marissa's side of the conversation."

"Well, he certainly can't think you are a ghost anymore," she said.

Marissa smiled. "No, he can't," she agreed.

They finished their meals and Marissa went to use the restroom before going back to work. Laura was sitting at the table drinking her tea.

Joe came down the hall at work. He was returning from lunch. As he came up to a mirror in the hall, he stopped suddenly. Laura's face had just appeared.

"Laura," he said.

"Joe," said Laura with a smile. "How did you do on your test?"

"I don't know, yet. I was a little distracted." said Joe. "How are you doing?" he asked.

"I'm okay," said Laura. "I'm here with my friend, Marissa. She saw someone in the mirror. She wanted to come back in and take another look."

"You haven't talked to anyone else in the mirror, have you?" asked Joe.

"No, only you," she said with a smile.

"I'm glad," said Joe.

"I have been dreaming about you. Only my dreams keep getting you mixed up with a Joe I knew in high school. I had a major crush on him," said Laura.

"What happened to him?" asked Joe.

"He was older and he didn't know I was alive," said Laura.

"It is hard to believe anyone would be able to ignore your beautiful face," said Joe.

"I was only in seventh grade. I had braces, freckles on my face and wore my hair in a pony tail," said Laura.

Joe laughed softly. "All of those things could not hide your true sweetness."

Laura blushed and laughed softly. "I haven't told my friend about you, yet. She has been so determined to find her true love. I decided to wait a bit," said Laura.

The mirror faded and Joe could no longer see Laura. She called out his name a couple of times, but there was no answer.

Marissa came back to the table. She looked around.

"Who were you talking to?" she asked.

"I'll tell you in the car. We had better go so you can get back to work," said Laura.

"Okay, talk," demanded Marissa, when they were in the car.

"I have been talking to someone in the mirror," said Laura.

Marissa looked shocked. "You did not tell me," she sounded hurt.

"I didn't believe it myself at first. I haven't seen him, although he can see me, so I don't know what he looks like. All I know is his name is Joe. He works as a typesetter and is going to the university at night after work," Laura paused to take a breath.

"Where does he live?" asked Marissa.

"I don't know," said Laura. "We have only had brief conversations. The mirror doesn't let us talk for long at a time."

Marissa grinned. "I know how the mirror likes to send out teasers. It seems as if it wants to keep us guessing."

"Yeah, Joe has a very busy schedule, with work and class, he does not have a lot of spare time," remarked Laura.

Marissa pulled to a stop in Laura's driveway. She hurried to help her inside. Laura stopped her from helping her upstairs.

"I can manage," she insisted.

"Okay, I have to get to work. We will talk more, later. I'll come over after work and we can talk some more about Joe and

Jed," Marissa left after making sure the door was closed and locked.

Laura sighed. She appreciated everyone trying to help her, but she was going to have to learn to take care of herself. She turned to head for the kitchen for a drink of water. She felt dizzy and light headed for a minute. She closed her eyes and leaned against the wall. When she opened her eyes, she saw a flash of light, then the light was gone, and it was dark again.

Laura turned and made her way back into the living room. She went to the sofa and sat down. She leaned back on the cushions and closed her eyes.

After she had rested for a while, Laura opened her eyes and sat up. There were no flashes of light. She sighed and reached for her purse. She took out her phone.

"Call, Dr. Holly Smith," she said.

The phone rang a few times before being picked up. "Dr. Smith's office," said a voice.

"This is Laura Sands. Could I speak to Dr. Smith, please?"

"Just a minute," said the voice.

"This is Dr. Smith. Hello, Laura. How can I help you?"

"Hello, Dr. Smith. I have seen flashes of light a couple of times, and I wondered if my sight might be returning."

"I need for you to come in and let me check you out. There is no way I can answer this without looking at your eyes. When can you come in?"

"I can get my friend to bring me in. She gets off work at 3 o'clock. Would 4 o'clock be alright?

"I'll be here. If you can't make it, just call the desk and leave me a message."

"Okay, Dr. Smith, I'll see you then."

Laura made a call to Marissa.

"Hello," said Marissa.

"Hi, I just wanted to see if you could take me to see my doctor when you get off work," said Laura.

"Sure, are you alright?" asked Marissa.

"I'm fine. She just wants to check me out," explained Laura.

"Okay, I'll see you then, bye," said Marissa.

Laura hung up with a sigh. She did not want to get everyone's hopes up when it might not mean anything. She lay back on the sofa to rest.

CHAPTER 4

*M*arissa arrived at Laura's house at 4:15. Laura was waiting for her. When she was seated in the car, Marissa looked at her. "What is going on? You did not say anything about a doctor's appointment earlier," asked Marissa.

"I called Dr. Smith to ask her about some flashes of light I have been having, and she told me to come in."

"You have been having flashes of light!" exclaimed Marissa. "Does it mean your eyes are getting better?"

"I don't know. The doctor said I would have to come in. She cannot give me an opinion without looking at my eyes first," said Laura.

"How many flashes have you had?" asked Marissa.

"Two," replied Laura.

"Well," said Marissa, stopping in the doctor's parking lot. "We can hope for the best."

"Yes," agreed Laura, as she exited the car and, with Marissa holding her arm, went into the doctor's office.

"Hello, Laura," said Nurse Melinda Leigh. "The doctor

will be with you shortly. Come with me, please." Laura and Marissa followed her back to an examining room. "Have a seat. The doctor will be right in," she said as she left.

"Real chatty," commented Marissa, after the nurse left. The girls took seats and waited.

"Hello, Laura," greeted Dr. Smith, as she entered.

"Hello, Dr. Smith. This is my friend, Marissa Embers."

Hello, Miss Embers, it is nice to meet you," said Dr. Smith, with a smile at Marissa.

"It is nice to meet you, too," said Marissa.

"Laura, you said you have had some flashes of light," Dr. Smith stated.

"Yes, twice. They were very brief. I thought I had imagined it the first time. Then, it happened again today," said Laura.

Dr Smith took out her small flashlight and, pulling her magnifier down over her eye, flashed the light into Laura's eyes. She examined both eyes thoroughly.

Dr. Smith sat back with a sigh. "Laura, I don't see any improvement in your eyes. They may still get better, but they have not improved so far," said Dr. Smith.

Laura shoulders slumped. She had tried not to get her hopes up, but she could not help hoping. Marissa frowned at the doctor. She hated to see Laura looking so defeated.

"How soon does improvement usually show?" she asked.

"Every case is different. All we can do is wait and hope," said Dr. Smith.

Laura got up and prepared to leave.

"Thank you for seeing me on such short notice, Dr. Smith," said Laura.

The doctor took her hand. "Anytime you have any concerns, you call me," said Dr. Smith. She walked Laura and Marissa out to the lobby and turned them over to a nurse to be shown out.

Laura was very quiet in the car on the way home. Marissa looked at her several times. She hated to see Laura so down.

"You want to go by Danny's on the way and check on our guys?" asked Marissa.

Laura sat up straight and smiled.

"Yes, I would really like to talk to Joe," she declared.

"The doctors don't know everything. Those flashes of light have to mean something. Don't give up," said Marissa.

"I'm not, I just got my hopes up, and she shot me down," said Laura with a smile.

Marissa pulled into Danny's parking lot and parked. As they were getting out of her car, a truck pulled up beside them and parked. Marissa looked up from helping Laura, straight into the eyes of Jed Hillard. She gave him a tentative smile.

Jed took his time climbing out of his truck.

"Who is here?" asked Laura.

"It's Jed Hillard," said Marissa. "Hello, Jed, this is my friend Laura. I'm Marissa." Marissa held out a hand for Jed to shake.

Jed looked at her hand like it might bite him, then reached over and accepted it for a handshake. A shock ran through both of them at their touch.

"Ouch," said Marissa, drawing her hand back.

Jed looked at his hand like he had never seen it before. He held out his hand to her again.

"You want to try again," he asked.

Marissa slowly reached for his hand. The shock wasn't as bad this time. It was more like a tingle. Jed held onto her hand. He looked at Laura.

"It is nice to meet you Laura," he said.

Laura smiled at him. "It is nice to meet you, too," she said.

"Can I escort you ladies inside?" he asked.

Marissa looked down to where her hand was still firmly

clutched in Jed's. She looked up at Jed and smiled. "Sure," she agreed.

Brian did a double take when he saw Jed enter with Marissa and Laura. He could see Marissa's hand being held firmly in Jed's. Brian smiled at all of them. "You girls are beginning to be regular customers," he said.

"There is no better place in town," said Marissa, with a smile.

"Yeah, you have the magic mirror," said Laura.

Brian looked at her curiously. "How does the mirror help you?" he asked.

Laura smiled. "You mean, because I can't see in it. My guy can see me and talk to me in the mirror," she replied.

All three of the group looked startled. Brian and Jed, because they didn't know it was possible and Marissa because she did not think Laura wanted anyone to know about her talking to Joe.

"Who is your guy?" asked Brian grinning.

Laura just smiled at him and did not answer.

"Could we get some ice tea?" asked Marissa. She looked down at her hand still firmly clutched in Jed's. Marissa looked up at Jed and smiled. He smiled back at her. He noticed her looking at their hands, but he did not let go. Her hand felt so right in his as if it had been waiting for his hand and belonged right where it was.

Brian brought the tea and set it on the counter. Marissa took Laura's arm to lead her to the mirror table. She smiled up at Jed.

"You will have to bring the tea," she said.

Jed let go reluctantly and picked up the two glasses. He followed the two ladies over to the table. After Laura was seated, Jed placed her tea on the table in front of her and Marissa showed her where it was. . Jed reached and took

Marissa's hand in his again. He felt the tingle go up his arm and saw Marissa shiver as his touch connected with hers. He smiled at her and she smiled back at him.

"We are going to sit at this table over to the side and give you some privacy," Marissa told Laura. "Just call if you need anything."

"Okay," agreed Laura.

Marissa and Jed sat at a table just a little way away from Laura, but it was in sight of the mirror. Laura sat back to drink her tea and wait.

"Have you ever been on a dairy farm?" asked Jed after they settled.

"No, I have lived my whole life in town. My dad is a teacher and my mom sells real estate. I have two sisters, but they are still in junior high school," said Marissa. "Have you always lived on the dairy farm?"

"Yes, it has been in my family for four generations. I have been in charge since my dad had a stroke. I love the place, but it does not allow for a lot of free time."

"Do you have any brothers and sisters?" asked Marissa.

"No sisters, one brother, but he left after we had a disagreement, and he hasn't been back," said Jed.

"That's too bad," said Marissa.

"Yeah, the whole disagreement was my fault. I accused him of something he did not do. He tried to tell me he did not do it, but I did not believe him. I punched him and he got up and left. It was the last time I saw him," Jed finished with a sigh. Marissa squeezed his hand in sympathy.

Jed shook off his sadness and smiled at her. "If anyone had told me I would be sitting here, holding your hand, and feeling like I had just won the lottery, I would have told them they were crazy,' said Jed with a smile.

Marissa smiled at him. I'm better than any lottery," she declared.

Jed looked at her seriously. "Yes, you are," he agreed.

Marissa looked over at Laura. She sighed. She saw Laura sit up straight and smile.

Joe had just got home from work and entered his room. He glanced in the mirror inside the front door and saw Laura there.

"Laura," he said and smiled.

"Hi," she said. "I am so glad you are here to talk to today," she said.

"What has happened?" he asked.

"I saw some flashes of light and I thought I was getting better. I went to the doctor and she said there was no improvement," Laura finished on a silent sob.

"I'm sorry. I wish I was there so I could hold you," said Joe.

"Me, too," said Laura.

"When you saw the flashes of light, it had to mean something. Maybe your eyes will only show improvement if they could check them when you see the flash. By the time you get to the doctor to be checked, your eyes may have adjusted back to the dark," said Joe.

"You think so?" asked Laura.

"I think you should not give up hoping," said Joe.

Joe looked past Laura to the table where Marissa and Jed were sitting. He stiffened.

"What town do you live in?" he asked.

"Sharpville," said Laura.

"You are in Danny's," stated Joe.

"How did you know?" asked Laura.

"I used to live there," said Joe.

"You lived in Sharpville," said Laura, startled.

"Yes, I grew up there," said Joe.

"Do you know the couple at the table close to you?" he asked.

"Yes, that is my friend Marissa and her friend Jed."

"Do you know Jed?" asked Joe.

"No, I just met him tonight," said Laura.

"Please don't say anything, but he is my brother," said Joe.

"Oh ... oh, I understand! Wow! Now, I know why you seemed so familiar to me, and why I had those weird dreams. You are the boy I had a crush on in junior high school," said Laura with a smile.

"You mean I'm the loser who did not notice what a wonderful prize was right under my nose?" said Joe in surprise.

"The very one," agreed Laura. "You did not know I was alive."

"Well, I know now, and I am looking forward to getting better acquainted with you. We have a very real connection."

"I'm looking forward to it, too. I hope when we do get to meet up, I will be able to see your face," Laura ended with a sigh.

"You said the mirror shows us our true love. True love does not come from the sight. It comes from the heart. You feel it inside," Joe said.

Laura looked up. There were tears on her face.

"Please don't cry. I did not mean to make you sad," Joe said.

"I'm not sad. I am happy. You say such lovely words. They make my heart feel loved," Laura smiled through her tears.

"I'm glad," said Joe.

The mirror faded out and Laura turned and smiled at Marissa. Marissa, seeing Laura looking at her quickly stood and went over to her table.

"Are you ready to go?" she asked.

"Yes, please," said Laura. "You can drop me off at home, and then you and Jed can have some time to yourselves."

Jed had come over to the table with Marissa. "I'll follow you over to Laura's. We can decide where to go from there," said Jed.

"Okay," agreed Marissa.

Marissa waited until they were in the car before she asked about Joe. "Yes, I talked to him. I think he is going to figure a way for us to meet. Talking to him really helped after the visit to the doctor," said Laura.

"When they stopped at Laura's house, Jed got out and came to the door with Laura and Marissa.

"It was nice to meet you," said Jed.

"I am glad we met," said Laura. "You be nice to my friend. She is a very special person."

Jed grinned at Marissa and Laura, even though Laura could not see his grin.

"I know she is special. I will always treat her that way," said Jed.

"Good," said Laura. "Good night."

"Good night," said Jed and Marissa.

As soon as Laura was inside, they turned and returned to their car and truck.

"I'll follow you home," said Jed taking her hand again. "Will you have dinner with me?"

"Dinner?" she laughed. "We just ate. You follow me home. We can talk about dinner there," Marissa leaned forward and gave Jed a light kiss. She pulled back quickly and entered her car.

Jed shook his head and hurried to his truck and followed her home.

CHAPTER 5

When Marissa pulled into her driveway at home, Jed pulled in behind her. Marissa got out of her car and walked back toward Jed's truck. He got out and came to meet her. Jed took her hand and pulled her close as soon as he was able. Marissa smiled up into his face. Jed leaned in and gently kissed her.

"About dinner," said Marissa.

"You are going with me, aren't you?" asked Jed.

"I would love to go with you, but this is my night to help out at the church. We have bingo for our older members once a week. I always help pass out cards. You could come with me. It won't last but a couple of hours and we could go out afterwards," Marissa looked up Jed pleadingly.

Jed smiled. "I guess I'm going to bingo. There is no way I'm saying good night, now." He pulled her close and kissed her again.

They pulled apart when the door opened. They turned and looked at the intruder.

"Marissa Embers, I'm going to tell Mom on you," said a very indignant teenager.

"Go ahead, Mavis, I don't care. What are you doing here?" asked Marissa "I thought you were spending the night with Karen,"

"I am. She will be here soon to pick me up," said Mavis.

"Jed, this impertinent youngster is my sister, Mavis," said Marissa.

"Mavis this is Jed," said Marissa.

"It is nice to meet you, Mavis," said Jed.

"It is nice to meet you," said Mavis flushing slightly.

Just then, Karen's Mom pulled to a stop. Karen opened the door and yelled for Mavis. Mavis grabbed her overnight bag from the porch and headed for the car. Marissa exchanged waves with Karen and her Mom as Mavis got in the car, stowed her bag, and fastened her seat belt.

Marissa laughed at the look on Jed's face after Mavis was gone.

"Welcome to the world of teenagers," she said.

"Does she always threaten to tell your Mom on you," asked Jed.

"Yes, she almost never follows through. She just wants attention. She is really a sweetheart," said Marissa.

Jed looked skeptical. Marissa laughed again. "Are you ready to go?" asked Jed.

"Yes, let me leave a quick note for Mom. When she sees my car, she might start worrying about me."

Marissa ran up the porch and unlocked the door. She wrote a quick note and left it on the table inside. She locked the door and hurried back to Jed, who was waiting patiently by the passenger door of his truck. He gave her another quick kiss before helping her inside.

They pulled into the church parking lot and parked. Jed took another kiss before helping Marissa out of the truck.

"This is the church my Mom took me and Joe to when we were young," said Jed.

"Yes, I know. I know your Mom. She comes into the drug store all the time to pick up your dad's medicine, and she almost never misses bingo," said Marissa.

"Mom plays bingo?" said Jed startled.

"Yes, every week. How could you not know?" asked Marissa.

"I guess I have been so busy on the dairy since Dad had his stroke, I just wasn't paying attention," replied Jed.

Marissa squeezed his hand. "It's time to start paying attention," she said.

They entered the church, and Marissa led the way into the rec room. She went to the table set up for her, and pulled out the bingo cards, stacking them in neat piles. She knew her piles would soon be scattered as the ladies tried to find a lucky card.

Marissa pulled up two chairs for her and Jed. They had barely got seated and pulled out the cash box before the ladies started arriving.

"Hello, Marissa, have you got a lucky card for me tonight," asked a spry, little, gray haired lady with a twinkle in her eye.

"They are all there, Mrs. Phillips. Take your pick," said Marissa with a smile.

"Who is your good-looking friend?" Mrs. Phillips asked. She smiled at Jed, who smiled back. He remembered Mrs. Phillips, but he supposed he had changed a lot since she last saw him.

"This is Jed Hillard," said Marissa.

"Jed!" exclaimed Mrs. Phillips. "You are Sara's boy."

"Yes, Ma'am, it is nice to see you again," said Jed rising and giving a hug to a very startled Mrs. Phillips.

"It is nice to see you back in church. Even if it is just for bingo," replied Mrs. Phillips. She picked up her cards, gave Marissa money for them, and hurried off to spread the word that Sara's son was there. Jed sat back down with a grin.

"You made her night," said Marissa with a smile.

"Jed, what are you doing here?' asked Sara Hillard.

"Hello, Mom," said Jed rising and kissing his Mom on her cheek. "I'm here with Marissa."

Sara looked at Marissa and smiled. "Hello, Marissa, how are you doing tonight?" asked Sara.

"I'm fine, Mrs. Hillard. How is Mr. Hillard doing?" asked Marissa.

"He's good. He and Andy were glad to see me go, so they could watch what they want to on the television," she said with a laugh. "How's Laura doing?"

"She is the same," said Marissa. "I wish there was some way to help her, but we just have to wait. At least she is starting to get out a little more."

"Tell her we will all be praying for her," said Sara. "I had better get my cards and get a seat before all of the good seats are gone. You behave yourself, Jed. Marissa is a special girl."

"I know, Mom. I'll be a gentleman," Jed declared with a hand over his heart. Marissa and Sara laughed at his antics. His mom went to get a seat and Jed sat back in his chair.

"Not too much of a gentleman, I hope,' said Marissa in a whisper.

Jed smiled at her and Marissa smiled back.

While Marissa and Jed were enjoying each other's company at the bingo game, Marsha and Cindy stopped at Danny's to visit Brian.

Danny came out and Cindy jumped into his arms. Danny was delighted with his honorary granddaughter's affection.

"Do you think you could hold some milk and cookies?" he asked Cindy.

Cindy nodded enthusiastically.

"Milk and cookies won't spoil her supper, will it?" he asked Marsha.

"No, it's fine," said Marsha grinning.

"I'll take her to the kitchen and see if we can talk Lany out of some cookies," said Danny.

Cindy took his hand and followed him through the swinging doors.

Brian put his arms around Marsha and pulled her close for a kiss.

After a very satisfying kiss, Brian pulled back slightly. "I have been thinking about Mary and Gary. I know their medical bills have been high, even with insurance. Gary is talking about taking a second job to help pay them. I would like to help out, but I don't want to offend his pride," said Brian.

"I know what you mean. They did receive a check from the police fund to help families of police officers, but I imagine it has been used up, said Marsha.

"We could spare the money. The Judge set up a trust fund for Cindy, so we don't have to worry about saving for her college. We still have a good amount left from the trust fund The Judge made for me when I was born. Even after buying a house and getting set up here we have quite a bit left. Is there any way we can find out how much they owe and pay it off without them finding out we paid it?" Brian asked.

"I'll see what I can find out tomorrow," promised Marsha.

"Is it okay with you for us to help?" asked Brian.

"I think it is a great idea, and I love you for thinking of it," said Marsha leaning forward and kissing Brian.

Danny and Cindy came back. Cindy still had half of a chocolate chip cookie in her hand. The rest was in her mouth, and she was chewing it around a big smile.

Brian and Marsha laughed.

"You had better close your mouth while you are chewing or your cookie is going to fall out, Little Miss," said Marsha.

Cindy quickly closed her mouth, but she was still grinning. She chewed and swallowed her cookie and took another big bite, while the adults watched her fondly.

Marissa and Jed watched the ladies play bingo. It was entertaining to see how serious they were about the game. When one of them cried, "Bingo," the whole group was quivering with excitement. Jed had never seen his Mom have so much fun. It was good to see how a small break helped her to relax and have fun. Marissa laughed when one woman stood and demanded attention for her bingo.

"I'm coming. Give me time to get there," said the official.

"Are you ready to go?" asked Marissa. "I don't think anyone else is coming."

"Yes, I am ready," said Jed taking her hand and helping her to stand.

They waved at Sara Hillard as they headed for the door. She waved back and gave them an approving smile. Once outside they made their way to Jed's truck, and Jed helped Marissa inside.

"Do you have any preference about food," asked Jed.

"I'm in the mood for pizza. The pizza place on Main has a buffet. I love mixing pizza and pasta with a salad," said Marissa.

Jed shook his head. "Okay, pizza it is, but next time we are going to a nice sit-down restaurant," he declared.

"So, there is going to be a next time," said Marissa smiling.

"Oh, yes, there is going to be a lot of next times," said Jed very seriously.

"I'm glad," said Marissa. She undid her seat belt, slid over closer to Jed, and fastened the middle belt. She leaned into his shoulder and laid her hand on his leg. Jed laid his hand on top of hers, and they both felt the shock go through them.

"I guess the universe is trying to tell us something," said Jed.

"Yes," agreed Marissa. "We are in for a shocking good time." Jed laughed and Marissa joined in.

"I don't mind the shock as long as I can hold on to you," said Jed.

"I love knowing you are holding my hand," said Marissa.

They stopped in front of the pizza place and went inside. The place was almost deserted, so they went toward the back and picked a table away from the people who were there. The waitress came over and they told her they were going to have the buffet. She took their drink orders and left. They went and filled their plates and when they returned to the table, the drinks were already there.

Marissa started in on her pizza. She took a big bite and chewed happily. She looked up to find Jed watching her eat. He had a smile on his face. "I can't help it. I'm hungry," she said.

"I love to see you eat," said Jed. "I hate seeing women picking at their food."

"I love my food too much to pick at it," said Marissa.

"Good," said Jed. He picked up his pizza and started eating.

"This is good," he declared.

"I know," agreed Marissa.

Marissa filled her fork with pasta and held it up before Jed.

He took the pasta into his mouth and chewed slowly. Marissa smiled at him and took a bite for herself. When she finished eating her pasta, she leaned forward, and Jed met her with a kiss.

"Now, that is the way to eat pasta," declared Jed.

"Ummmmm, I agree," said Marissa.

They continued eating the pasta, with a kiss between each bite, until it was gone. The pizza soon disappeared also.

"Do you want me to refill our plates?" asked Jed.

"No, I'm stuffed," said Marissa.

Jed took the check to pay at the front and, with his arm around Marissa, made his way out to his truck.

They drove around for a while. Neither of them wanted to say good night. They were enjoying just being together. Finally, Jed headed toward Marissa's home. Marissa sighed and looked at Jed when he parked behind her car.

"I had a great time tonight," she said. "Thank you for coming to Bingo with me."

"I would have gone anywhere just to be with you, but I really enjoyed being at the Bingo game. I saw a different side of Mom. One I haven't seen since Dad had his stroke. Thank you for taking me and opening my eyes," Jed gathered into his arms and kissed her soundly and deeply.

"You're welcome," said Marissa breathlessly.

She lay her head on his chest and enjoyed being held close to him. Jed tightened his arms around her. They sat there, enjoying their closeness.

Finally, Marissa stirred. "I had better go in. I have work tomorrow," she said.

"What time do you get off work?" asked Jed.

"I get off at 4 o'clock tomorrow," she said.

"I'll pick you up here at 4:15, okay?" asked Jed.

"Okay," agreed Marissa with a smile.

Kissing her one more time, Jed got out and went around the truck to open her door. Marissa slid over and let him help her out. Jed put his arm around Marissa and walked her slowly to her front door. At the door, he turned her to face him and kissed her again.

"I'll see you tomorrow," he promised.

"Yes," agreed Marissa. She smiled as she took out her key and opened her front door. She turned and smiled at Jed before closing and locking the door.

Jed headed for his truck. He was walking on air. He hadn't ever felt this good. He smiled as he headed his truck toward the farm.

When Marissa turned around, she was startled to see her dad sitting on the sofa. He was working on some papers. Marissa smiled and she sat down beside him.

"Hi, Dad," she said.

"Hi, yourself, did you have a good night at bingo?" he asked.

"Yes, I went out for pizza with a friend afterwards," said Marissa.

"Is he the young man Mavis saw you kissing in the front driveway?" he asked with a smile.

"Yes, he was. I see Mavis has been busy. It was Jed Hillard. I saw his reflection in the mirror at Danny's. He is my true love," declared Marissa.

Her dad looked at her for a minute, and then sighed. "Is he the Hillard who owns the dairy farm just outside of town?" he asked.

"Yes, he is. His mom is a member of our church. She was at bingo tonight. His dad is disabled because of a stroke. He's partially paralyzed. His mom is very nice," said Marissa.

"Just take things slowly. Make sure you know what you are

getting into, before getting in too deep," he said. "I don't want my little girl getting hurt."

"I'm not a little girl anymore, Dad. I am all grown up."

"To me, you will always be my little girl," said Saul Embers. "You will just have to endure it."

"I love you, Dad," said Marissa, hugging his arm.

"I love you, too," said Saul. "Now, get to bed and let me finish grading these papers so I can get some sleep, also."

"Good night, Dad, said Marissa.

"Good night, sleep well," he said, his attention going back to his papers.

Marissa rose and headed upstairs to her room. She was hoping to dream of Jed.

CHAPTER 6

*M*arsha called their lawyer first thing the next morning. She explained about Laura's medical bills and how she and Brian would like to pay them anonymously. The lawyer said he would look into it and get back to her. Marsha called Brian at Danny's, where he was working on inventory. She told him the lawyer was looking into Laura's medical bills and he would let them know as soon as he had the information.

"Thanks for checking. I love you," said Brian.

"I love you, too," said Marsha.

Jed called Marissa early.

"Hello," whispered Marissa.

"I'm sorry I woke you up," said Jed.

"Jed," said Marissa. "Is anything wrong?"

"No, I just wondered if you would like a tour of the dairy

farm. When I pick you up, we could drive out and look around. Afterwards, I could take you out to dinner."

"I would love to see the farm," agreed Marissa.

"Good, go back to sleep. I'll see you at later," said Jed.

"Yes," agreed Marissa, turning over and closing her eyes. Her eyes popped back open. Marissa grinned. "I am going to the dairy farm."

She jumped up and started going through her closet to find the perfect outfit to wear to work. It could not be too dressy if she was going to visit the farm in it. She needed some comfortable shoes. She changed her mind several times before she settled on the perfect outfit. She had tan slacks, tennis shoes, a grey blouse and a sweater, in case it became cool. She laid her outfit out and went to make coffee and toast. She loved toast with her early morning coffee.

While Marissa was worrying about what to wear on a tour of the dairy farm, Marsha was receiving a call from her lawyer. When she finished talking to him, she smiled and quickly called Brian at Danny's.

"Hello," said Brian.

"Hi, I just got off the phone with our lawyer," said Marsha.

"What did he have to say?" asked Brian.

"He said he talked to the person in charge of the fund to help policemen and their families. He said we can donate money to them designated for the Sands family bills. It can be done anonymously. He can handle the transfer. The total is not as bad as I thought. We can pay it off and add in some more to help with future expenses. What do you think?" she paused for an answer.

"I think we should tell him to get it done. The sooner it is set up, the sooner Gary and Mary can stop worrying," said Brian.

"Okay, I'll tell him to go ahead and set it up. I love you," said Marsha.

"I love you, too. Thanks for going along with my idea," said Brian.

"You are a wonderful man Brian Dane. I am proud to be your wife," said Marsha.

Brian flushed slightly. He smiled.

"I am just so grateful you came to find me and we got a second chance at love. Now, we have Cindy and life is great. We have to pass the love on and show our gratitude for all of our blessings," Brian replied.

"I am glad we have this chance, too. Are you going to be home early tonight?" asked Marsha.

"I don't know when I'll be finished here. Was there a reason I need to come home?" asked Brian.

"I wanted to talk to you about something," said Marsha.

"Are you still at home?"

"Yes, I had an errand to run, so I took the morning off," Marsha replied.

"I'll take a break and be there in a few minutes," said Brian.

Brian walked through the door a few minutes later. Marsha met him as he entered and went straight into his arms.

"As much as I enjoy being greeted like this, I don't have long," said Brian.

"I know," sighed Marsha.

"I went by the drugstore and picked up a pregnancy test this morning. Congratulations Mr. Dane. You're about to be a father again," said Marsha with a big grin.

Brian smiled back at her and he squeezed her tightly and swung her around.

"I'm glad you are happy about it," said Marsha. "I wasn't sure you were ready for another baby."

"I love you and I don't care how many babies we have. You can have a dozen if you want to. It will just mean more to love."

"I don't think I am ready for a dozen," laughed Marsha. "One or two more will be nice. I love being a mom, as long as I have you by my side as a dad."

They spent the next minutes in a very satisfying way. Brian called Danny and told him he was taking the rest of the morning off. He had to celebrate being a dad again. Danny was delighted he was going to have another honorary grandchild and after congratulating them told Brian to take all the time off he needed.

It was a very happy couple who took a call, later in the day, from their lawyer telling them the fund for the Sands was set up and ready to go.

Gary Sands received a call on his police radio while he was out on patrol. He was asked to go by the office, and talk to the lady in charge of the police fund for families, when he finished his shift.

Gary Sands was smiling ear to ear when he later left the office and headed home. He went into his home and, finding his wife in the kitchen, picked her up and swung her around before hugging her tightly.

Mary hugged him back and smiled at how excited he was.

"What has happened?" she asked.

"The police fund has paid Laura's medical bills and given me this check for $5000 for future expenses," said Gary.

Mary looked at the check with disbelief.

"Wow," she said. "How could they afford to do this?"

"They said it was from an anonymous donor. The person wanted to help, but did not want to be in the limelight. I am just grateful they picked us to help," he said.

"Me, too," agreed Mary hugging Gary again.

Laura, who had been on her way downstairs, heard her mom and dad talking about the bills being paid. She did not want to interrupt their celebrating, so she turned and quietly went back upstairs.

Laura sighed. She wished she could talk to Joe. Next time she talked to him, she was going to give him her phone number, so he could call her. She could not spend all of her time in Danny's hoping the mirror would let them talk. She could not call Marissa. Marissa had plans with Jed. She had not told Marissa about Joe being Jed's brother.

Laura hoped Joe and Jed could put the past behind them. With Marissa being with Jed, things could be awkward for her and Marissa. She did not want to lose her best friend. She had been friends with Marissa since kindergarten. She fell in love with Joe in seventh grade. She did not want to lose either to them. Laura sighed. Why was life so hard at times?

A very excited Marissa went into Jed's arms, beside his truck, when he picked her up after work. They kissed, and Jed helped her into her seat. Going around to the driver's side, Jed climbed in and grinned at Marissa. He unfastened her seat belt so she could move into the middle, closer to him. Marissa smiled and moved closer. She fastened the middle belt and placed her hand on Jed's leg. After they were on their way, Jed placed his hand on hers and squeezed.

"I'm glad you wanted to see the dairy farm," said Jed.

"The farm is important to you. Of course I want to see it," declared Marissa.

It did not take long before they were pulling into the parking lot in front of the barn. Before they got out, Jed turned to Marissa. "I need to explain to you about my engagement," he said.

"You are engaged?" said Marissa, startled.

"No," said Jed quickly. "I was a few years back. I broke it off, because she was cheating on me. Unfortunately, I did not find out how she was in time to save my relationship with my brother. When I saw her snuggled up to Joe, she claimed Joe was coming on to her. I believed her, even though Joe said she was coming on to him. I punched him out and he just looked at me and left.

A few days later I found Sharon in my office getting too familiar with one of my workers. I broke the engagement and made her leave. I realized I was relieved to be done with her."

"Something similar happened to me," said Marissa.

"You were engaged?" asked Jed.

"No, I was at the prom with a boy I liked a lot. I thought he really liked me too. We were double dating with Laura and her date. Well, he disappeared and he was gone so long, me, Laura and Jeff went looking for him. We went outside the dance room and started down the hall. We had only got about halfway down the hall when we heard a noise coming from the room where coats were stored. I opened the door and there was Tad with the town tramp. Both of them had their clothes half off.

"I just stood there, stunned. Tad started yelling at me telling me it was my fault. He said if I put out, he would not have gone elsewhere. I just turned away in disgust. Laura went right up to him. She looked him right in the face and told him he was a fool and did not deserve me. She started to turn away and changed her mind. She doubled up her fist and hit him in the stomach as hard as she could. She looked at the girl with him, and then shook her head in disgust. We all left. Jeff drove us to my house and dropped us off. I think he was scared to face Laura alone. I took Laura in and gave her an ice pack for her hand and got out some ice cream. We ate ice cream and laughed about the look on Tad's face when he realized he had been caught."

Marissa looked at Jed who was trying very hard to hold back his laughter. "We all have our skeletons, some worse than others. They are in the past. They need to stay there. We are the future," said Marissa with a smile.

Jed pulled her into his arms and kissed her. "Let's go look around," he said. He took her through the milk house where the milk was stored. Then, they went through where the feed and hay were stored. The barn was full of cows being milked. They stood at the end and watched the workers go from cow to cow, checking machines.

The guys all smiled and waved at them but did not stop working to come over. Jed took her outside and showed her the pasture where the cows were turned loose when they had been milked. There was another pasture for cows waiting their turn to be milked.

They returned to the truck and Jed pulled up in front of the house. He wanted her to meet his dad. Sara Hillard met them at the door as they came onto the porch. She smiled at Marissa. "Come on in," she said holding the door wide.

"Hello, Mrs. Hillard," said Marissa.

Jed leaned forward and kissed his mom's cheek.

"Call me Sara," she said. "Come on in and meet Ron and Andy."

She led them into the living room, where two men were playing a game of checkers.

"Hi, Dad," said Jed going over and patting him on his

shoulder. Ron's smile looked more like a grimace with one side of his face paralyzed.

"Hi, Andy," said Jed. "This lovely lady is the love of my life, Marissa Embers."

"Hello," said Marissa with a smile.

"I have been showing Marissa around the farm," said Jed.

"Would you like to stay for supper," invited Sara. "I have a pot roast with potatoes cooked."

Marissa looked at Jed inquiringly. He looked back leaving it up to her. Marissa shrugged her shoulders. She needed to get better acquainted with Jed's family.

"Okay," she agreed. "Can I help?"

"It's ready, but you can help me set the table," said Sara.

Marissa and Sara turned and left the room. Jed followed them.

"Jed you can get out glasses and ice for tea," said Sara.

She handed Marissa silverware and left them to start putting food on the table.

"You don't mind, do you?" Marissa asked Jed quietly.

"No, I want you to be happy and I want you to get to know my family. I just wish Joe was here," said Jed.

Sara, coming into the dining room with food, looked startled. "Maybe, when he finishes school, he will come home." said Sara.

"Joe's in school?" asked Jed.

Sara looked down. She had not meant to say anything.

"Yes, he is taking night classes. He works in the day to pay for tuition," she said.

Marissa looked thoughtful. "Sara, by any chance, would Joe be working as a typesetter?" she asked.

Sara looked up shocked. "How did you know?" she asked.

"Because, my friend, Laura, has been chatting with

someone named Joe in the magic mirror, and he is working as a typesetter and taking evening classes."

"How can she talk to him in the mirror when she can't see?" asked Sara.

"He can see her," replied Marissa. "Wow, I can't believe her Joe in the mirror is your Joe. Laura had a major crush on your brother since seventh grade. He did not notice her, and she never tried to get his attention, but she was very much in love with him."

"If Joe is in love with Laura and Laura with him, then there is a good chance he will come home!" said Jed.

Sara looked thoughtful. Then, she smiled. "I hope you are right," she said. "I would love for my son to come home."

Jed went over and hugged his mom. "Me, too, Mom, me, too," he said.

Marissa took a paper out of her purse and wrote Laura's phone number on it. She gave the number to Sara.

"If Joe asks for it, I want you to have Laura's phone number. He can call her instead of waiting on a connection from the magic mirror. Sometimes it is hard to get to Danny's. Especially, when you can't drive yourself," Marissa said with a smile.

Sara took the number and put it in her pocket. "If I hear from Joe, I will have it ready," replied Sara. "Jed, tell Andy and your dad supper is ready."

Jed turned and went to help Andy bring his dad to the table. When he came back, he seated Marissa and sat in the chair next to her. He took her hand and, ignoring the shock, held it under the table.

Marissa smiled at him and looked around the table. She caught Sara's eye and smiled at her.

They bowed their heads, and Andy said the blessing. Then, they started passing food around. Andy helped Ron with his.

"This is delicious," said Marissa after taking a couple of bites of pot roast.

"Mom is a great cook," agreed Jed.

Sara flushed slightly. "It's just plain food," she said.

"Sometimes, plain food tastes best," said Marissa. "I am going to have to get you to give me some tips."

"I would love to," said Sara, smiling at Marissa.

Jed squeezed Marissa's hand and smiled at her.

After they ate, Andy took Ron to his room. Jed and Marissa helped Sara clear the table and load the dishwasher.

We have to go," said Jed. "Marissa has to work tomorrow."

"I had a lovely time. Thanks for supper. It was great," said Marissa giving Sara a hug.

"You are welcome anytime," said Sara. "It was nice to have company."

"Good night, Mom. I won't be long, but don't wait up. Get some rest," said Jed kissing his mom on the cheek.

"Good night, Jed. Take care of Marissa. She is special."

"I know, Mom. I will," said Jed looking at Marissa as she flushed slightly.

When they were in the truck on the way to town, Marissa looked up at Jed and smiled.

"Thank you for taking me to the farm. I had a great time," said Marissa."

"I wanted you to see what it was like. The farm is a large part of my life. I want us to be together, so you needed to know what to expect, said Jed.

"As long as we are together, I can handle anything. Where we are does not matter. Being with you matters," said Marissa.

Jed pulled the truck to the side of the road and took Marissa in his arms and proceeded to kiss her passionately.

CHAPTER 7

The next day at work, Marissa could not stop smiling. She even chuckled a couple of times when she thought of the deputy sheriff's car pulling in behind her and Jed on the side of the road. The light from the car made them pull back and stop kissing. Jed rolled down his window as the deputy came to his door.

"Is anything wrong, Jed?" asked the deputy sheriff, Mike Griffen.

"No, we were just talking," said Jed. "Everything is fine."

Mike grinned at him, then smiled at Marissa. "How are you doing, Marissa?" he asked.

"I'm fine, Mike. How is Mary Jane? Is her cold any better?" asked Marissa.

"Yes, she is better. She has been up for a couple of days. I imagine she would like a couple of more days off, but my mom is bringing the kids back day after tomorrow, so rest time is over," Mike laughed.

"I'm glad she is better," said Marissa. "Tell her I said hello."

"I will. You guys take care. No more talking on the side of the road," chuckled Mike.

He left with a wave, and Jed started the truck and headed to town. He looked curiously at Marissa.

"What is it?" asked Marissa.

"Do you know everyone in town?" he asked.

"Just about," said Marissa with a shrug. "I know a lot from school. Then, many more from church, the ones left, most of them come into the drug store. I have been working there for over two years. I like to get to know people."

Jed smiled. "I'm glad you had the mirror to show you we were made for each other."

"Me too," said Marissa hugging his arm and leaning on his shoulder.

Marissa turned back to her customer and smiled.

"Here you are, Mrs. Hanks," she said, handing a bag over the counter.

"Thank you, Marissa. You sure look happy today," she remarked.

"Yes, I am. It is a beautiful day," agreed Marissa.

"It wouldn't have something to do with Sara's son, would it?' Mrs. Hanks inquired with a wink.

"It just might," agreed Marissa. "Have a nice day, Mrs. Hanks."

Mrs. Hanks patted Marissa on her arm and took her bag. "I'll see you soon, dear, take care," she said.

Mrs. Hanks left to spread the word about Marissa and Jed. She wanted to be up on the latest gossip. She was not malicious. The ladies were all very fond of Marissa. They liked Jed, too. They were only wishing the best for both of them.

~

Tilly and her best friend, Macy, entered the house. They stopped when they saw Laura sitting downstairs on the sofa.

"Hi, Laura," said Tilly. "Macy is going to spend the night with me tonight."

"Hi, Tilly, hi, Macy," said Laura. "Are you two getting ready for the prom?"

"Yes," said Tilly. "We don't have to go to school tomorrow. They let us be out to decorate and get things ready for the prom. Mom arranged hair appointments for us, and Macy brought her dress so we can get dressed here. Stephan and George are going to pick us up here."

Laura smiled. "You make sure Mom gets lots of pictures. I'm sure Macy's parents will want some. The guys may want copies also."

"I'll tell her," agreed Tilly. "Thank you for letting me use your prom dress," said Tilly.

"The dress is yours," said Laura. "I don't need it and I'm sure you will put it to good use."

Tilly hurried over and hugged Laura. "You are the best sister in the world," she said.

Laura laughed. "I'm your only sister," she said. Tilly and Macy laughed with her. "You girls have a good time," said Laura.

Tilly and Macy said bye and hurried upstairs to Tilly's room to plan for the prom. They were both on the decorating committee and were going to spend the morning helping decorate. They had a hair appointment at one, so they had to have all of their plans in order. They were making lists and talking to other members of the committee on the phone. Everything seemed to be in order, but they were not taking any chances. They wanted everything to be perfect.

"Who do you think will be picked for king and queen?' asked Macy.

"Probably, Angie and Jack," said Tilly. "Everyone I talked to said they were voting for them"

"Yeah, I guess so," agreed Macy. "They do seem to be the most popular."

"Well, I don't care who wins. I just want to enjoy my prom and my date with Stephan. I did not think he was ever going to ask me out. School is almost over and we will be going to college, I have been waiting a long time for him to notice me," sighed Tilly.

"I think he noticed you. He is just shy. At least you will get to dance with him," said Macy.

"Yes, I will," agreed Tilly hugging herself and flopping back on her bed.

"How did you get George to notice you?" asked Tilly.

"I wore the sexiest clothes they would allow in school and hung around where he could not help but see me," laughed Macy. "It did not take long for him to start drooling."

Tilly laughed. "I'm glad it worked," she said. "It's just not my style. I would not be able to get out of the house with sexy clothes. Dad would send me back to change. Did you know Mrs. Dane and her husband are going to be chaperones?"

"Yes, I heard. I also heard she is dropping the self-defense class, she is teaching at the school. She is getting someone else to take over next year," said Macy.

"Yes, I know. I heard she is expecting and does not want to take a chance on hurting the baby," said Tilly.

"Oh, I hadn't heard about that. I am glad. She and Mr. Dane make wonderful parents," said Macy."

"Yes, they do," agreed Tilly. "Cindy is a doll. I love babysitting her when I get a chance."

While Tilly and Macy were busy with planning for the prom, Mac was asking Laura's help with his homework. The homework was finished quickly, and Mac turned on the television. There was a comedy on. Mac started describing to Laura what was going on while they listened to the dialogue. They were both laughing at Mac's commentary. They were laughing so much they did not hear their mom come in. She looked into the living room but did not enter. She was so glad to see Laura enjoying herself again.

It had been a while since she saw her children just sit and laugh with each other. She went on to the kitchen and wiped the tears off her lashes. Gary's arms came around her from behind.

"Why the tears?" he asked.

"They are happy tears," she said turning in his arms. "I was just so happy to see Laura and Mac having so much fun."

"Yeah, it was nice. They did not even notice me coming through," said Gary.

"I know," said Mary. "They did not see me either."

"I heard Tilly and Macy upstairs," said Gary.

"Yes, Macy is spending the night. They are planning for the prom," said Mary.

Mary gave Gary a kiss and shooed him out so she could start supper.

Gary went to take a shower and change into something besides his uniform. Mac waved at him when he passed the living room, but did not interrupt the show he and Laura were watching.

Marissa finished her work day and went home to shower and change before Jed came to pick her up. She was so happy. She had to pinch herself to make sure she wasn't dreaming. All the times she had gone to Danny's to look in the magic mirror, she had never envisioned being so happy. She and Jed had not been together for long, but she was in love with him, and she thought he felt the same. They were both in this relationship for the long haul. Marissa sighed. Love was great. If only Laura and Joe could get together, and Laura could get her sight back, everything would be perfect.

Jed was parked in front of her house when she pulled into the driveway. Marissa stopped her car and headed for Jed's truck. He got out and held his arms open to receive her as she walked into them and they closed around her. After a very satisfactory greeting, Marissa leaned back and smiled at Jed.

"Do you want to come in and wait while I shower and change?" she asked.

"Sure," said Jed. "Are you sure your folks won't mind?"

"You can wait in the living room. They may as well all get used to having you around. I plan on being in your life for a long time," said Marissa.

Jed gave her another kiss and hug. He turned to follow her inside. He held onto her hand. He was getting used to the tingle he got when they touched. He would miss it if it went away. Inside the door Marissa showed him into the living room and offered him the television remote. With a quick kiss, she hurried to her room to shower and change.

Gary came into the living room. Mary had sent him to tell Laura and Mac supper was ready.

"Hey you two," said Gary. "Are you ready to eat?"

"Yeah, I'm starving," declared Mac. Gary and Laura laughed. Mac was always starving. Mac hurried out, headed for the dining room. Gary came over to where Laura was sitting. Laura took her cane and rose. She was light-headed and dizzy for a minute.

Gary took her arm. "Are you okay?"

"I'm fine," said Laura. "I guess I must have got up too fast."

"Have you had dizzy spells before?" asked Gary.

"No, I have had a couple of light flashes, but the doctor said there was no improvement," said Laura.

"Hmmm," said Gary.

"What?" Laura asked?

"It just seems to me your doctor is dismissing things too easy. Light flashes have to mean something. Maybe we need to get a second opinion," said Gary.

"Can we wait a little while? I really don't feel up to all of those tests again right now," said Laura.

Gary looked at her for a minute while he thought about her request.

"I'll talk to your mom, and we will check into it. Relax, we are not rushing anything," said Gary.

"Okay," said Laura as Gary held her arm and walked toward the dining room. Everyone else was already seated and Gary helped Laura to her seat before taking his chair. They all bowed their heads for the blessing, and they started passing the food around.

Tilly was sitting next to Laura, spooning out portions of the food onto Laura's plate. Finally, Laura held up her hand.

"Stop, I can't eat all of this. Don't give me any more," she said.

"It is really not much," said Tilly. "Meat is at 12 o'clock. Potatoes and gravy are at 6 o'clock, peas are at 3 o'clock, and corn is at 9 o'clock. Your roll is on the right side and tea is right above it."

"Thanks, you make everything easy," said Laura.

Gary and Mary looked at Tilly in amazement while she was talking to Laura. "How did you know all of this?" asked Mary.

"I read up on it," said Tilly. "I'm thinking about taking some classes on teaching students with disabilities in college," said Tilly.

"You should do great," said Laura.

"Thanks," said Tilly. "I never thought much about it before, but since Laura's accident, I realized how much help I could be. It would be so much better than just teaching. I feel like I could really accomplish something good." Everybody was smiling at Tilly.

"We are so proud of you," said Mary.

"Yeah, my sister, the over-achiever, you are a lot to live up to," declared Mac.

"Don't worry, Mac," said Gary. "You still have a few years to decide what interests you."

"I know, Dad," said Mac. "I am proud to have such smart sisters. I just have no idea what I am going to do with my life. It's frustrating at times."

"I know," agreed Gary. "I was the same way at your age. Then, a policeman came to our school recruiting. I was hooked. I am sure something will pop up for you when the time is right."

Mac shrugged. Mary and Gary smiled at him. Tilly punched him in the arm and Macy just smiled at him. Mac flushed slightly at all of the attention.

Laura had been quietly eating small bites of food, so she would not mess up and embarrass herself. She didn't say much. She had to concentrate, so she could keep everything straight.

Besides, she had her mind on Joe. She was wondering when she would get another chance to talk with him. Since she found out he was Joe Hillard, she was wondering if they would ever get a chance to have a life together. With Joe and Jed on the outs, Laura did not know what to expect.

Laura sighed. Why did life have to be so complicated? What good was the magic mirror if it showed you your true love and you could not be together?

"Have you girls decided on a theme for the prom?" asked Mary.

"Yes, Ma'am," said Macy. "It's going to be "SOAR ON A MOONBEAM and SEE OUR FUTURE STARS". We have a large moon with a beam of light coming out from it. We have made large shiny stars with a graduate's picture on each one and a lot of twinkling stars scattered around. We already have most of the decorations. We just have to decorate the gym."

"It sounds beautiful," said Laura.

"Yes, it does," agreed Mary. "You girls have outdone yourselves."

Both girls flushed slightly and smiled at the praise.

CHAPTER 8

The next day, Tilly and Macy hurried to the school to help with the decorations. They made sure to leave in time to make it to their hair appointment. After being pampered with hair, nails, and makeup, they headed to Tilly's house to finish getting ready.

They raided Laura's jewelry box for earrings and Laura gave Tilly the shoes to match her dress. The girls were so excited they could not be still.

Mary made them both take a few minutes and eat a sandwich and drink a glass of tea. She told them they could not dance all night on empty. Although snacks and punch were being served, when the students started dancing, they sometimes ignored them.

The time finally arrived. Both girls were ready and showed their dresses to Mary and Gary. Even Mac agreed they looked fantastic.

Mary got her camera ready and took some pictures of the girls before their dates arrived.

Stephan and George arrived together. Stephan was driving,

and he had gone by and picked George up on the way. They had wrist corsages for the girls, but they almost forgot to give them to the girls when they walked in and saw how beautiful they were.

Stephan stood speechless staring at Tilly.

"You look beautiful," he stammered.

"Thank you," said Tilly. "You look very handsome."

"Thank you," said Stephan smiling. "This is for you." He held out the corsage for her to put on. Tilly held out her hand and let him slide it onto her wrist.

George and Macy were having a similar conversation. They both were smiling and staring at each other.

"Okay," said Mary. "It's picture time."

She held up her camera and had the couples pose for pictures. She took some pictures of each couple and some of all four together. She took so many pictures, Tilly started to get impatient. "Come on, Mom. If we take any more pictures, we will be late for the prom."

Everyone laughed and Mary put away her camera. She gave Tilly and Macy a hug and told them to have a good time. She reminded them Marsha and Brian were going to be there if they were needed. Both girls promised to remember and let their dates help them into the car. When everyone was seated, the girls waved as they drove away.

Mary went inside and took the card out of her camera and started downloading pictures to print. She soon had a stack of very nice prom pictures. She made two copies of all of them. She made two extra copies of the individual couples, in case the guys wanted some. She got out a couple of albums and made Tilly and Macy each a prom picture album.

She was having a good time, but she was getting weepy again because her babies were all growing up. Gary came over and hugged her. He could see how it was affecting her.

"Just be patient. Before you know it, you will have grandchildren to spoil," he said.

"If you are trying to cheer me up, it's not working," she said, but she smiled and hugged him back.

Meanwhile, the group arrived at the gym. They found a parking place and made their way to the front door together. As they entered, each couple stood in the center of a large star for their picture to be taken.

"There shouldn't be any more pictures," Tilly reassured Stephan.

"I don't mind," he said squeezing her hand.

They waited for Macy and George to get their picture taken, and they all entered together. The guys looked around in amazement. The girls smiled in satisfaction at their expressions. The gym really did look great. The band on the stage started to play, so the guys turned to the girls and led them onto the dance floor.

It was a slow dance, and Tilly was enjoying being held close to Stephan. She glanced over and saw Macy enjoying her dance with George. Tilly lay her head on Stephan's shoulder and tuned everything out except him. She was finally dancing in his arms.

They danced a couple of more times before they took a break and wandered over to the refreshment table. Tilly and Macy waited while Stephan and George fetched them a cup of punch each. They drank their punch and wandered around speaking to their fellow students.

Marsha and Brian danced by and waved at Tilly. Tilly waved back with a smile. She looked around. Everyone was having a good time. Most of the couples were dancing. The band was playing a faster number and Tilly was content to stand beside Stephan and watch.

Stephan took her hand and squeezed it. She turned her head and smiled at him.

Tilly noticed a group of boys off to one side. They came without dates and were laughing and talking together. They were getting a little loud, she thought with a frown. Tilly saw a monitor go over and speak to the boys. She must have told them to keep the noise down. They quieted some after the monitor left them.

Another slow song started playing and Stephan turned to Tilly with a smile. "Shall we?" he asked.

"Yes," agreed Tilly taking his hand and rejoining the dancers.

One of the boys from the corner came over and tapped Stephan on the shoulder to cut in. Stephan looked at Tilly. She shook her head.

"Sorry," said Stephan. "The lady said no."

He danced Tilly away from the boy. The boy stood staring for a minute, and then angrily made his way back to his friends. They were laughing at his rejection. He looked at Stephan and Tilly with a glare. He blamed them for his embarrassment.

Tilly and Stephan were oblivious to his glare. They were only aware of each other.

The next two hours was a dream come true for Tilly and Stephan. Tilly danced in Stephan's arms and they chatted with class mates. The principal made speeches a couple of times. They listened to him and went back to dancing. Marsha and Brian came by when they were resting and complimented them on the decorations.

Everyone seemed to be having a great time. Macy and George stopped and talked to them at the refreshment table. Tilly could tell Macy was really happy.

"I wish I had got up the nerve to ask you out before now," said Stephan.

"Why didn't you?" asked Tilly curiously.

"You always seemed to have so many friends around, I didn't think you could be interested in going out with me," said Stephan.

"I was very interested," said Tilly. "I didn't think you even noticed me."

"I noticed you. How could I not notice the most beautiful girl in the school?" He declared. Tilly grinned. "Are you going to college?" asked Stephan.

"I've got a scholarship to State," said Tilly.

"Good," said Stephan with a big grin. "I'm going to State, too."

Tilly smiled. "Really?" she said. "Wonderful."

"Yes, isn't it. We can still see each other and maybe help with homework," said Stephan. "We can get to know each other better."

"What is your major?" asked Tilly.

"I'm taking business management and computer science," said Stephan. "What about you?"

"I'm going to be studying how to teach students with disabilities," said Tilly.

"You will do great," said Stephan.

"So will you," said Tilly. "With both of us studying, we will ace everything," agreed Tilly.

Stephan hugged her closer. "I am so glad you are not going to be at a college way away from me."

"Me. Too," said Tilly. Tilly looked around to see if she could spot Macy. She didn't see her anywhere. Stephan noticed her looking around.

"What is it?" he asked.

"I was looking for Macy. I don't see her anywhere," said Tilly.

"I'm sure she is around. We will spot her soon," said Stephan.

"Yes," agreed Tilly with a grimace. "I wanted to get her to go with me to the ladies' room. I don't like going out in the hall by myself."

"I'll walk out with you and wait in the hall for you," said Stephan.

"You don't mind?" asked Tilly.

"No, come on," Stephan took her hand and led her toward the door to the hall.

They told the monitor where they were going and went down the hall to the ladies' room. Stephan waited out in the hall as Tilly went inside.

Tilly hurried to use the facilities and get back, she did not want to keep Stephan waiting too long. When she was washing her hands, she heard talking. She hurried out into the hall.

She saw the boy who had asked her to dance and two of his friends. He was confronting Stephan while his two friends held his arms on each side. Stephan was pulling, trying to get loose. They laughed at him.

"Not so smart now," sneered the boy. He pulled his fist back to hit Stephan.

"What's going on here?" demanded Tilly. "Let him go."

The boy turned to her with a sneer. "You think you are too good to dance with me," he sneered.

"Let Stephan alone. I will call the monitor," said Tilly.

The boy grabbed her arm tightly. "You aren't calling anybody," he declared breathing in her face.

"You are drunk," said Tilly holding her head back.

"Not drunk, I only had a few drinks to loosen up," he sneered.

"Let her go," demanded Stephan.

"I don't think so. We are going to get better acquainted," said the boy pulling Tilly closer.

"No, we are not," said Tilly. She brought her leg up between his legs as hard as she could.

"Owwww!" he squealed as he turned Tilly loose and folded up in a ball on the floor. He was holding himself and moaning. His two friends loosened their hold on Stephan and he used both arms to pull them around so they bumped into each other. He then proceeded to punch; first one, then the other, in the jaw. They both joined their friend on the floor.

The monitor looked out and, seeing the boys on the floor, she talked into a button on her lapel. She hurried over and was soon joined by Marsha and Brian.

"What's going on?" asked Marsha.

"These boys jumped Stephan while I was in the ladies' room," said Tilly.

"They had been drinking," said Stephan.

"Did you put them out?" asked Brian.

"I only got these two. Tilly took care of him," he said pointing at the ring leader.

Brian looked at the moaning boy curiously. "What did you do to him?" he asked Tilly.

"He wouldn't turn me loose, so I brought my leg up between his as hard as I could," said Tilly.

"Ouch," said Brian with a grimace. Marsha and the monitor grinned.

"My dad told me if I ever had to use the knee, to make sure I did it hard. He said if I didn't, the person would just get mad and hurt me," said Tilly.

"He was absolutely right," said Marsha giving Tilly a hug. "You did good. So did you Stephan. Now, why don't you two rejoin the dance while we get some medical help and cooling off time for these three?"

73

Stephan took Tilly's arm and guided her back into the dance. They started dancing and tried to ignore all the talking going on around them. Macy and George danced over to them and suggested getting some punch. Tilly and Stephan followed them to the refreshment table. Stephan kept his arm around Tilly. He seemed to want to be close to her. They both needed to cool off and maybe punch would help.

Tilly told Macy what happened. There were several students around and word soon spread through the group. The boys had been terrorizing other girls and boys. The others had not wanted to start anything at the prom, so the boys had been getting away with it. Stephan had several guys come by and clap him on the shoulder and say, "Good Job." Tilly had her share of good wishes, too. The girls seemed to wish they could have put that boy down.

They went back to dancing, and the principal came to the microphone to tell everyone to be sure and vote for king and queen. He also reminded everyone they were underage, and no alcohol was allowed on school property.

The next few dances were slow, and Stephan and Tilly were enjoying just holding each other and swaying to the music.

The principal cut in again and called for attention. "We have a count in for king and queen. The vote was unanimous. I don't think it has ever been unanimous in the history of our school," he said.

"The prom queen is Matilda Sands, and the prom king is Stephan Salvo. Come on up and be crowned."

Stephan led Tilly toward the stage. They were both astonished. They had no idea they were even being considered. The principal put the crowns on first Tilly and then Stephan. Everyone cheered and clapped.

The principal went to the microphone again. "I should tell

you this is a write in vote. Everyone tore up the old votes and wrote in the new votes, so we know you are the student's choice." Everyone cheered again. There were phone camera's flashing and the photographers were taking pictures.

"Now everyone, let's let our king and queen have their dance," said the band leader.

Stephen and Tilly went down off the stage onto the floor and the band started playing. Stephan grinned at Tilly and she smiled back into his eyes. "My queen," he said.

"My king," replied Tilly.

He hugged her closely and they continued to dance.

CHAPTER 9

"Would you like to go to the movies with me Friday?" asked Stephan. They were on the way to Tilly's house after the prom.

"I would like that," said Tilly.

Stephan and George opened the doors for the girls and escorted them to the front door. Both guys pulled the girls close for a good night kiss.

"I had a great night, if you forget the fight," said Tilly with a laugh.

"Me, too," said Stephan. "I'll pick you up at 6 o'clock Friday. We can get something to eat first."

"Okay," said Tilly. She leaned in for another kiss before going inside.

Macy and George had been saying good night in a similar fashion. Macy hurried to join Tilly going inside. The guys left, and Tilly and Macy hurried upstairs quietly before they awakened anyone.

The next morning, everyone met in the dining room for a

late breakfast. Even Laura was there. They all wanted to hear how prom night went.

"I hear we are in the presence of royalty," said Mary.

"What?" asked Mac.

"It seems Tilly and Stephen were crowned prom queen and king," she replied with a smile.

"Congratulations," said Laura. "Did you get to keep the crown?"

"No, but there are lots of pictures," said Tilly.

"Marsha told me you had a little trouble," said Gary.

"Yes," said Macy. "Some boys were drinking and tried to hurt Stephan and Tilly. They took care of it though."

"How did you take care of it?" asked Gary.

"Well, he wouldn't get his hands off me, so, I kneed him in his family jewels. Stephan knocked the other two out," said Tilly.

"You girls are dangerous at proms. It's a good thing you don't have any more," said Gary with a smile.

"What are you talking about?" asked Tilly.

"Your sister punched Marissa's date in the stomach at their prom," said Gary.

"What!" exclaimed Tilly? "Why would you punch Marissa's date?' asked Tilly.

"We caught him with his pants down with another girl in the coat closet at the prom. Marissa was so upset she just turned and left. I told him he did not deserve Marissa and punched him in the stomach. We went over to Marissa's house, and she made me an ice bag for my hand and we celebrated with ice cream," Laura laughed. "The boy I went to prom with was so scared of me, he turned and went the other way anytime he saw me coming afterwards."

"Wow," said Mac. "I need to get you girls to give me some pointers."

Gary laughed. "I'm glad everything turned out alright. Marsha said the boys have been turned over to their parents. They were checked out by medics. Other than bruises and some pain, they will be fine."

"I'm glad they are alright," said Tilly. "I hope someone gets them some help with their drinking."

"Marsha said they agreed to go to rehab. It was suggested by the principal and the parents agreed," said Gary.

"I found out Stephan is going to State when we graduate," said Tilly, changing the subject.

Macy smiled. "George is going to State, too."

"Alright," said Tilly giving Macy a high five. Everyone smiled.

"Laura," said Mary. "Your dad and I talked it over and decided to get a second opinion on your eyes. We have an appointment on Monday. I have the day off, and I will take you in to see him."

"Okay, thanks Mom," said Laura.

"Have you had any more dizzy spells?" asked Gary.

"No, but I did see a flash of light when I first woke up this morning. It was gone very quickly," replied Laura.

"We will see what the doctor has to say on Monday," said Mary.

"Alright," agreed Laura.

In Kansas City, Joe was getting concerned about Laura. He had been looking in every mirror he passed. He had not talked to her in several days. He was hoping she was alright. Being worried about Laura was distracting him from studying. He was studying for finals, and he wanted to do well. He needed to find out if Laura was alright.

Joe thought about it for a while, then, he decided to call his mom and see if she knew anything about Laura. He wanted to let her know about his graduation. It was only a month away. She might be upset if he did not let her know about it.

Joe dialed the number at home and waited for it to ring. It rang three times before it was answered.

"Hello," said Sara Hillard.

"Hi, Mom, it's me, Joe."

"Joe, I'm so glad you called. How are you doing? How are your classes going?"

Joe laughed.

"I'm doing good. I'm studying hard for finals. The classes are going okay. Graduation is in a month. How are things at home?"

"Your dad is the same. Andy takes good care of him. Jed has a new girlfriend. She is a real nice person. She goes to our church and helps out at bingo each week," said Sara.

"I'm glad he found someone," said Joe.

"He's really sorry about how he treated you before," said Sara.

Joe sighed. "It's in the past, Mom. Let's leave it there. I know Sharon had everyone snowed. I'm just glad he woke up before he married her."

"Yeah, me, too," agreed Sara.

"Mom, do you know a girl named Laura who is blind?" asked Joe.

"Yes, I know Laura. She's a good friend of Marissa, Jed's girlfriend, and she was working in the drug store until she had her accident," said Sara.

"Do you know if she is doing okay? I haven't heard from her in several days and I am worried about her," said Joe.

"As far as I know she is. Just a minute, Marissa gave me Laura's phone number. Let me get it."

Sara looked in the book by the phone where they kept numbers. She found Laura's number and returned to Joe. She read off the number to Joe and he wrote it down.

"Are you coming home after graduation?" asked Sara.

"I don't know. I applied for a job on the paper there. I haven't heard from them, yet," said Joe. "Even if I don't move back, I'll be back for a visit."

'I'm glad. I love you, son. You take care of yourself," said Sara.

"I love you, too, Mom. Give Dad a hug from me, and I'll see you all soon," said Joe.

When they hung up the phone, Sara had tears running down her face. Jed coming in the back door looked at her with concern. He hurried over and put his arms around her.

"What's wrong?" he asked.

"I'm just so happy," said Sara. "Joe just called. He was worried about Laura. I gave him her number. He said he was coming home after graduation. He doesn't know if he is staying, yet, but he will be back for a visit."

"I am glad he's coming. Maybe we can patch things up between us. When is graduation?" asked Jed.

"He said it was in a month. I didn't get the exact date," said Sara.

"It should be easy enough to find out," said Jed. "Maybe we can surprise him and go to his graduation."

"I would like that," said Sara, smiling.

As soon as Joe hung up the phone with his mom, he dialed Laura's number. He waited impatiently for an answer.

"Hello," said Laura.

"Hi, Laura," said Joe.

"Joe!!" exclaimed Laura.

"How did you get my number? I was just wishing I had given it to you," said Laura.

"I got it from my mom. She said Marissa gave it to her. I haven't heard from you and I was worried. Are you alright?" asked Joe.

"I'm okay. Mom is taking me to another doctor Monday. She wants to get a second opinion about my eyes," said Laura.

"Good, I will keep my fingers crossed for you," said Joe.

Laura laughed. "It may be hard to set type with your fingers crossed."

Joe laughed, too. "When I have to set type, I'll keep them crossed in my mind."

"Thanks, I am so glad you called. It's hard to get to Danny's now that Marissa and Jed are together," said Laura.

"I'm glad they found each other. I told Mom I would be back for a visit after graduation. I have applied for a job at the local paper, but I haven't heard from them, yet. I just have to wait and see," said Joe.

"I'm glad you will be back then. When is graduation?" asked Laura.

"It's a month away. There is a chance I may be the class valedictorian," said Joe.

"Oh, Joe, that's wonderful. I am so happy for you," exclaimed Laura.

"It's not definite, yet," said Joe.

"I'll keep my fingers crossed for you," laughed Laura. Joe laughed, also. "I was just wondering, how you feel about working in broadcasting?" asked Laura.

"I haven't thought about it, but it would be interesting," said Joe.

"Just before my accident, I overheard a person from our local station talking in the drugstore. He was saying he was going to have to leave in a few months and he wanted to give the heads up to start looking for a replacement. I don't know if they are still looking, but it might be worth looking into," said Laura.

"I'll check into it," agreed Joe. "Thanks for the tip."

"You are welcome. I want you close," said Laura.

"I want you close, too," agreed Joe. "You're on my mind all of the time. Do you suppose a person can fall in love through a mirror?" asked Joe.

"I don't know. I was already in love with you. I haven't even considered anyone else since seventh grade, whispered Laura.

"Oh, Laura," whispered Joe. "It makes my heart ache not to be close enough to hold you."

"Me too," said Laura.

"Have you got my number, so you can let me know how your doctor's appointment goes?" asked Joe.

"It's in my phone. I'll program it to voice call when we hang up," replied Laura.

"Okay, I had better go. Don't forget to call. I love you," replied Joe.

"I love you, too. I will call. Don't worry. I'll be alright," said Laura.

Laura hung up the phone and programmed Joe's number for voice. She then lay back on the bed with a happy smile on her face.

Joe hung up and headed for class. He received many curious looks for the smile on his face. It made everyone a little happier to observe such happiness in another.

Laura called Marissa.

"Hello," said Marissa.

"Hi, Marissa, I know you are with Jed. I won't keep you. I just wanted to thank you for giving my number to Joe's mom. He just called, and we talked," said Laura.

"Slow down. Jed hasn't got here, yet. I'm glad Joe called. Are you alright? I haven't seen you for a few days, and I was wondering," said Marissa.

"I'm great. Mom is taking me to a different doctor on Monday. She wants a second opinion. Joe's phone call was the best medicine I could have had. I love him, Marissa," declared Laura.

"I know you do. I have been around you since you first saw him in seventh grade. You were standing, staring at him with your mouth open. I had to turn you around before you embarrassed both of us," Marissa laughed at the memory.

"I wasn't that bad," protested Laura laughing with her.

"Yes, you were," said Marissa. "I have to go. Jed's here. I'll talk to you soon. Let me know what the doctor says."

"I will. Thanks again," said Laura.

Laura hung up and smiled. She was glad her friend and Jed had found each other. She wanted Marissa to be happy.

CHAPTER 10

*J*oe finished his class and decided to look into the television station in Sharpville. He did a search for it on his computer. He found a web page for it and clicked onto it. It looked like the station had good reviews. It also had a nice following. He scrolled down and saw they were advertising for a newscaster and part time reporter.

Joe had been submitting articles to the newspaper where he worked as a typesetter. A number of them had accepted and printed in the paper. He decided to apply for the job and send a sample of his work, including a copy of his college resume with the information about his standing in class and consideration for valedictorian. He finished up the application and, sitting back with a sigh, sent it to their e-mail.. Now, he could only wait and hope to hear back from them.

Joe smiled. It had been so good to talk to Laura. It would be better if he could see her. He could not imagine what it was like for her, not being able to see. He could only pray she would get her sight back. If she didn't, he was still going to convince her to make a life with him. They belonged together. He had to convince her to take a chance with him.

Joe smiled. He could always tell her the magic mirror picked them to be together. After all, it was not every day when a person was shown their own true love. It was something to cherish and tell your grandchildren about. Joe laughed. He was getting a little ahead of himself. He and Laura had to get together and have children before they could think about grandchildren.

He wondered what Laura would say if she knew he was already planning their lives. She would probably tell him to slow down and enjoy being in love. Joe turned over and tried to sleep. After all, tomorrow was going to come early and it would be a long day. Just one more month, and he would graduate. It had been a struggle, but he made it. With a sigh, he closed his eyes and slept.

Laura was sleeping, also. She had been thinking about Joe. It would be great if she could see him graduate. She was so proud of him for possibly making valedictorian of his class. Even though he said it was not final, she was sure he would make it. Laura sighed and turned over. In her sleep she could see. She saw Joe as she last saw him. It had been at his high school graduation. Laura never told anyone about going to see him graduate. It was the last time she saw him.

He had left town before she had a chance to see him again. Now, she might never get the chance to gaze into his eyes and see the love he said he felt. Her heart ached with love for him. She called out in her sleep.

"Joe," she whispered.

"Laura," said Joe.

"You can hear me," she said. "Yes, I can feel your heart beating so fast," said Joe. "I am so glad to be able to feel you with my heart. It knows we are meant to be together."

"Your heart is beating fast, too," said Laura. "I can see your face. You are beautiful."

"Not beautiful, handsome," replied Joe.

"To me, you will always be beautiful," smiled Laura.

"Are you sleeping?" asked Laura.

"I suppose so," said Joe. "It feels so real. I was wishing to be able to be close to you just before I went to sleep. I guess we are dreaming. I love you and I am glad we can at least, have this moment."

"Me, too, I was wishing I could see your face, and then, there you were. I have never had such vivid dreams before. At least, not that I remember," said Laura.

"I don't remember having any dreams about girls before. You are the only girl I have ever dreamed about," said Joe.

"I had some dreams about you when I was in high school, but you were not aware of me. It was like I was off in the distance looking at you. I guess it was like real life. I was always at a distance looking at you wistfully," Laura sighed.

"I'm not at a distance anymore. I am right here, loving you and aching to be close to you," said Joe.

Laura felt her eyes fill with tears.

"Don't cry," said Joe.

"I am crying happy tears. I love you so much. It is hard for me to believe you finally see me and love me, too. My heart is full to overflowing. This is a great feeling." Laura smiled through her tears.

Joe took her hand and squeezed it. They fell out of the dream and into deep sleep. Their hands were still holding each other.

The next morning, when Laura awoke, her hand was still lying where she placed it to hold Joe's hand, and it felt warm, like it had been nestled in his.

Joe opened his eyes and looked at his hand. He could still

feel the touch of Laura's hand in his. He could feel the tingle of their connection.

Joe sighed. It was going to be a long month.

When Joe left work the next day, he went by his room to eat before going to class. He only had one test tonight. While he was eating, he opened his computer. He found an e-mail from the broadcasting company in Sharpville. It said the position was still open and they would like to talk to him further. They gave a number for him to call. The number was to be used during business hours. He looked at his watch. It was too late to call back today. He would have to call in the morning before going to work. Joe hurried off to class. He was excited and cautiously optimistic.

Meanwhile Tilly and Macy joined the cleanup crews in the gym. The students were all excitedly talking about the prom and planning for graduation. Everyone was ready to finish graduating and hurry off to colleges all around the country. They were, almost all of them, ready to try their wings. They were sure they would do great on their own.

Tilly smiled at Macy. She and Macy were excited about going to college, too, but mostly because Stephan and George would be there also. They were both mature enough to know they still needed their parents' guidance. They hurried to get through and go. They both had plans for the night and wanted a little time to make sure they looked their best.

Sharon's parents were still living outside of Sharpville. Mr. and Mrs. Sering had not been told the details of Jed and

Sharon's breakup. Sharon just told them she changed her mind. Shortly after the breakup, Sharon hooked up with a traveling salesman and left town with him. She stayed with him until she managed to get to a larger town and find someone with more money. She managed to have several relationships since then.

Sharon called her mother regularly. She wanted to keep communication open with her in case she needed money. Her mother would send her a little along to help her out.

When Sharon called her mother this time, her mother mentioned Jed was seeing someone seriously. Sharon was startled. She was fine with Jed being alone. She was sure she could go back and hook up with him when she decided to settle down. If he was seeing someone, she didn't like the sound of it. Maybe, she needed to make a visit to see her folks and check things out. She considered Jed her's. She was not going to let some country bumpkin take her future away from her. Sharon packed her clothes and, putting everything in her car, headed for Sharpville. Sharon called her mother and told her she was on her way. Her mother was thrilled. Sharon told her not to tell anyone she wanted it to be a surprise.

Sharon arrived in Sharpville late at night. She was tired after the long drive, so, taking in one bag, she went in and greeted her mother and father. Her mother prepared her room, and it was ready for her. She told them goodnight and crashed.

The next morning, her mother spoiled her with a large breakfast. Sharon did not do it justice, but she ate enough to not hurt her mother's feelings. After breakfast, she told her mother she was going to scout around town and see what changes there were.

Sharon parked on Main Street, and started walking down the street, looking in shop windows. She waved at a few people when they recognized her. She smiled to herself. With the way gossip traveled in this town, the news of her return would soon reach Jed.

Jed was oblivious to her return. He was having lunch with Marissa. They finished up and were walking back to the drug store, when they were interrupted.

"Hello, Jed," said Sharon.

Marissa and Jed had been so wrapped up in each other; they had not noticed Sharon until she spoke.

"Sharon," said Jed. "What are you doing here?"

"I'm visiting my parents," she said.

Marissa knew who Sharon was as soon as Jed said her name. She looked at Sharon curiously. Her lifestyle was beginning to show. She was beginning to show her age.

Jed started to go around her and continue to the drug store.

"Aren't you going to introduce me to your friend?" asked Sharon.

"No," replied Jed.

"I'm Sharon, Jed's former fiancée," said Sharon to Marissa.

"I know," said Marissa. She turned and looked at Jed. She could tell he did not want to stay and talk to Sharon. She smiled at him. "It's a miracle you didn't catch anything being with her," she told Jed with a smile. "You did get checked out afterwards, didn't you?"

Jed looked at Marissa and grinned. "Yes, I did. The doctor gave me an all clear," said Jed.

"Good," said Marissa. They ignored a very indignant Sharon and continued on to the drug store. Once there, Jed turned Marissa in his arms and kissed her soundly. There were several whistles and catcalls, but they ignored them all.

"You are amazing," said Jed.

"I know." agreed Marissa.

Jed laughed and hugged her one last time before letting her go into work.

Sharon headed for home. She was fed up with this town and its people. She could not wait to leave.

Jed went by Danny's for a drink before heading home. He sat down at the bar. Brian and Danny were both behind the bar. Brian gave Jed his drink. He looked serious. He looked at Danny as if for guidance. Danny shrugged his shoulders. Jed watched them and smiled.

"I know Sharon is in town," said Jed. "Marissa and I bumped into her on the way to the drug store after lunch."

"How did it go?" asked Brian.

Jed smiled. "It went fine. She stopped us and wanted to be introduced to Marissa. I said no, so she tried to introduce herself. Marissa looked at me and smiled. I was worried for a minute. Then Marissa told me I was lucky I did not catch anything being with Sharon. She asked me if I had been checked out. I told her I had an all clear from the doctor. Sharon just stood there with her mouth open while we left and went on to the drug store."

Brian and Danny looked at Jed, then at each other. They burst out laughing. Jed laughed with them. When they finally could keep a straight face, Brian looked at Joe.

"You found yourself one heck of a lady. You are very lucky. She reminds me of Marsha. We don't let ladies like them get away. You had better make sure she knows how you feel about her."

"I plan on doing just that," agreed Jed.

With a wave of his hand he headed for the door. He had been neglecting the farm lately. He needed to put in a little time there before it was time to pick up Marissa.

Marissa went to work with a smile on her face. She had several customers come through just to let her know about Sharon. She smiled gently to all of them and sweetly thanked them for the information.

She and Jed did not have to worry about Sharon. They had true love on their side. The magic mirror did not make mistakes. Sharon could just go back where she came from. Jed belonged with her now.

Sara Hillard came in to get her husband's prescription filled. She heard about Sharon from one of her friends. She wanted to reassure Marissa, but she could see Marissa did not need any reassurance. She was fine. Sara breathed a sigh of relief. She was so glad Marissa and not Sharon was with Jed.

Marissa gave Sara a hug and told her not to worry. After she left, Marissa called Jed and told him to reassure Sara.

"Thanks, Sweetheart. I'll talk to her and I'll see you after work. I love you," said Jed.

"I love you, too. I'll see you later," Marissa hung up satisfied with Jed's response.

CHAPTER 11

On Monday, Laura and Mary were early for the doctor's appointment. They had gone by the hospital and picked up Laura's x-rays to take with them. They turned the x-rays over to the receptionist when they checked in. The receptionist took the x-rays back to the nurse and asked them to be seated. She said the doctor would be with them shortly.

They waited for about twenty minutes before the nurse called them to come back. They went into a room and Laura explained about the flashes and dizziness. The nurse made notes and told them the doctor would be with them shortly. They had only been waiting a few minutes when the doctor entered the room.

"Hello, I'm Doctor Ellias," he said smiling at Mary.

"Hello, Doctor Ellias, I'm Mary Sands and this is my daughter, Laura. Thank you for seeing us."

"I understand Laura has been seeing light flashes," he said.

"Yes," replied Laura. "I have had some brief flashes of light and a dizzy spell."

"Let's take a look and see what is going on," said the Doctor.

The doctor pulled a machine over to Laura. He placed it in front of her eyes and adjusted it to her height. He then shone a light in her eyes. While he was studying her eyes, the camera in front of her eyes was taking a video of everything and showing it on a screen mounted across from Laura and the doctor. The doctor studied her eyes from all angles and then sat up with a sigh.

"Laura, there is a lot of bruising around your optic nerve. There looks like there may have been a slight improvement with some of the bruising healing. That might be why you had flashes of light. There is no way to know if the bruising will continue to heal. If it does, you will get at least some of your eyesight back. I can give you some drops to put in your eyes. They will keep your eyes lubricated and help with the healing. They won't make you see, but they will keep your eyes from getting worse. From what I have seen, you have a good chance of recovering at least some of your sight, but there are no guarantees," the doctor sat back and waited for Laura to think about what he had said.

"Thank you, Doctor. At least we have some hope. No one else was even the least bit encouraging," said Mary.

"Yes, thank you, Doctor," said Laura.

The doctor wrote out a prescription for the drops and gave it to Mary.

"If there is any change, get in touch with me at once, otherwise, make an appointment at the front desk for a month from now," He got up, patted Laura on the arm and shook hands with Mary before leaving.

Mary helped Laura up and they went out the door to find a nurse waiting to guide them to the front desk. They made the appointment and went outside to the car. Mary and Laura were both thoughtful. This doctor had given them some much needed hope.

As they were driving home, Laura's phone rang. She got it out of her purse to answer it.

"Hello," said Laura.

"Hello, Beautiful, how did the doctor's appointment go?" asked Joe.

"Joe!" exclaimed Laura. "It went alright. The doctor said I had bruising around my optic nerve. He said there had been some healing, making me see the flashes of light. He doesn't know how much better it's going to get, but he said I stand a good chance of getting at least some of my sight back."

"I am happy for you. Whether you see or not, you will always be my true love. Nothing is going to change that," said Joe.

"Oh, Joe, I love you, too," said Laura. Startled, Mary glanced at Laura.

"I put in an application at the station there in Sharpville," said Joe. "I heard back from them and they want to interview me. The manager is going to be in Kansas City next week. He wants to talk to me while he is here. I guess he wants to see how I will show up in front of the camera."

"I am so excited for you. It would be great if you managed to get the job here in town. I bet your folks would love it, too," said Laura.

"Don't say anything, I haven't told them, yet. I did not want to get their hopes up, in case I don't get the job," said Joe.

"Okay, but you let me know as soon as you hear anything," said Laura.

"I will," agreed Joe.

Laura became aware the car was parked and her mother was waiting to help her inside.

"I have to go, Joe. We are at home," said Laura.

"We, who?" asked Joe.

"My mom and I," said Laura. "Mom drove me to see the doctor."

"Okay," said Joe. "I love you."

"I love you, too," said Laura. She hung up the phone and waited for her mom to speak.

"Joe, who?" asked Mary.

"Joe Hillard, He's Jed's brother," said Laura.

"Where was he calling from?" asked Mary.

"Kansas City, He's living and working there while he goes to college," said Laura.

"How long have you known him?" asked Mary?

"Since seventh grade," said Laura. "He didn't notice me then. The magic mirror matched us to each other more recently."

"How could the mirror match you when you can't see?" asked Mary.

"I was sitting in front of it waiting for Marissa, when Joe started talking to me. I could not see him, but he could see me," said Laura.

"I see," said Mary. "We need to go inside. We can talk more when we get out of the car."

She and Laura got out and headed for the door to their house.

They barely got inside when Mary's phone rang. Mary answered and began to explain to Laura's dad about the doctor's visit and what hope he gave them.

Laura wandered on into the living room and sat on the sofa to wait. She knew her mom had more questions.

Just as Mary finished talking to Gary and entered into the living room where Laura was waiting, Tilly and Macy came in the front door. They saw Laura and Mary and joined them to find out about the doctor visit. Laura told them all the doctor told her. Mary added to the story and told Tilly about the doctor saying not to give up hope.

"Did you know about Laura's feelings for Joe?" asked Mary, looking at Tilly.

"Yeah, sure," responded Tilly, looking surprised. "She used to write his name all over her things. She had a real crush on him when she was in high school."

Tilly looked at her mom curiously, and then she looked at Laura.

"Why?" she asked.

Laura flushed a little when Tilly mentioned how she felt about Joe in high school.

"I'm not talking about high school," said Mary. "I'm talking about now."

Tilly looked at Laura surprised. "You hooked back up with Joe?" she asked.

"Yes," said Laura.

"I thought he left town," said Macy.

"He did. He is going to college in Kansas City," said Laura.

"Oh," said Tilly. "How did you two get together?"

"We got together in the magic mirror at Danny's," said Laura.

"The magic mirror," said Tilly and Macy together.

"It really works?" asked Tilly.

"Yes," agreed Laura. "It really works. Marissa saw Jed in the mirror, also."

"How could you see Joe in the mirror when you can't see?" asked Tilly.

"I was sitting in front of the mirror waiting on Marissa and Joe saw me. We started talking and realized we knew each other," said Laura.

"Wow," said Tilly. Mary sat quietly listening. She was finding out everything she wanted to know without having to ask any questions. "When are you guys going to be able to get together?" asked Tilly.

"Joe is graduating in about a month. He may be moving back to Sharpville if his job situation works out. We have to wait and see. It seems 'wait and see' is a popular response to everything," sighed Laura.

"What are you girls up to?" asked Laura.

"We have been at the school getting ready for graduation," said Tilly. "We tried on our caps and gowns. Everything is coming together nicely."

"How long is it until graduation?" Laura asked.

"We have a week and a half left," said Macy.

"Have you sent in your college acceptance?" asked Laura.

"Yes, it is all taken care of. I have even received a packet back from them with dorm assignment. Macy and I are going to be sharing a dorm room," said Tilly.

"When did you get the packet?" asked Mary.

"It came in today's mail," said Tilly.

"Could I see it?" asked Mary.

"Sure, it is in my room. I'll run up and get it," said Tilly hurrying out of the room and up the stairs. They all sat waiting for her return.

At least, Mary had been distracted from worrying about her and Joe, thought Laura.

Tilly brought back the packet, and the girls and Mary went through it, discussing everything in it, while Laura sat quietly listening.

Finally, Laura excused herself and went upstairs to rest. She was unaware of Mary watching her with a worried expression as she left.

Tilly saw her mom watching Laura and tried to reassure her.

"She's going to be alright, Mom," said Tilly.

"I know. I can't help but worry. She has been through so much the last six months. I hope she is not going to get hurt with her feelings for Joe," she said with a sigh.

"We have to trust Laura to know her own feelings. She would not like us second guessing her," said Tilly.

"I know. I'm not thinking about Laura's feelings. I'm sure they are real. I'm worried about Joe's feelings. He had better watch out if he hurts Laura. Your dad would make him wish he hadn't," said Mary fiercely.

Tilly laughed. "I'm glad Dad likes Stephan," she said.

Mary looked at her startled. Then, she smiled. He had a few worries, but he has laid them to rest," she said.

"Good," said Tilly. "Do you need help with dinner?"

"No, it's mostly in the crock pot. I'm just going to make some bread to go with it. I'll call you when it is time to eat."

Mary headed for the kitchen and the girls headed for the stairs.

CHAPTER 12

*L*any, the cook at Danny's, was taking the trash out behind Danny's Bar and Grill. He dumped the trash into the dumpster and closed it with a bang. He turned to go back inside but stopped when he heard a noise between the two dumpsters.

He turned and went back to look. There between the dumpsters was a small child. He looked scared. The dumpster noise must have frightened him. He was sitting on a dirty blanket and was dirty and probably hungry.

Lany knelt down to talk to him. He was trying to reassure him so he would not be so scared.

"Hey there young fellow," said Lany holding out his hand. The baby just stared at him and ignored his hand.

"I won't hurt you. I have something to eat inside. If you come with me, we can find you something to eat and get you warmed up," said Lany.

The baby held out a hand to Lany. Lany took his hand gently and lifted the boy into his arms. He took him into the house and, without putting him down, poured him a glass of milk and took out a batch of fries that was done. He sat, and holding the child in his lap, started letting him drink the milk. He put the fries in front of him so he could eat one. He encouraged him to take a piece of it.

The boy drank half the glass of milk before stopping. He then reached for a piece of the fry. He ate it quickly and reached for another.

Brian came into the kitchen. He looked amazed when he saw Lany sitting feeding the boy.

"What have we got here?" asked Brian.

The boy leaned back closer to Lany. He looked scared, again. "It's alright," said Lany, soothingly. "I found him out back, between the dumpsters," said Lany. "Could you call it in while I feed him? He acts like he is starving."

"Sure, I'll call Marsha. She can send someone out," said Brian.

Danny came into the kitchen and had to be told what was happening while Brian called and filled in Marsha. Marsha reported it while Brian stayed on the phone. When he hung up, he told Lany and Danny that Gary would be there shortly.

Danny put some more fries in to cook and took the rest of his order to the front. He promised his customer he would bring the fries when they were cooked.

Gary came into the kitchen through the back door a few minutes later. He wanted to look around where the baby was found first. When he came in, he had the blanket the baby had been lying on. When the baby saw the blanket, he leaned forward and held out his hand for it.

Gary took the blanket over to him and held it out to him.

"Hey there, Dude. Is this your blanket?" asked Gary softly. "What's your name?"

"Sam," whispered the baby.

Sam held his arms out to Gary, and Gary lifted him into his

arms. Sam started playing with the badge on Gary's uniform. He smiled at Gary. Gary smiled back.

Marsha came in with the women from Child Protective Service. She came over to Gary and smiled at Sam. He smiled back after looking at her badge.

"I think he is familiar with policemen. You need to put in a call and see if a policeman has reported a missing child," said Gary.

"We will have to take him to a group home until we find out where he belongs," said Mrs. Parrish from CPS. "We don't have any foster homes open to care for him right now."

Gary held Sam a little closer to him. He did not like the sound of the CPS solution at all.

"Mary and I can be his foster parents until we find out where he belongs," said Gary.

"You are not certified to be a foster parent," said Mrs. Parrish.

"Well, you can get us certified," demanded Gary. "This little fellow is not going into a group home." He held Sam closer to him. Sam lay his head on Gary shoulder and closed his eyes.

"Poor little fellow is exhausted," said Brian.

"We can't approve of what you suggest, Officer Sands," said Mrs. Parrish.

"Why not?" asked Gary.

"It's not proper procedure," she replied.

"We are not talking about procedure," said Gary. "We are talking about what is good for a child."

"Let me see if I can help," suggested Brian.

"Sure," agreed Gary.

Brian dialed a number on his phone and waited for an answer.

"Hello, Brian. How are you and Marsha doing?" asked The Judge.

"We are fine, Judge. I have a little problem I am hoping you can help me with," said Brian.

"What is the problem?" asked the Judge.

"We found a small child in the alley behind Danny's. My friend Gary Sands, who is a police officer, wants to take care of the child until we find out where he belongs. The Child Protective Services lady, Mrs. Parrish, said it was not proper procedure. She said the child would have to go to a group home because there is no foster care home available. Can you help?" asked Brian.

"Let me talk to Mrs. Parrish, Brian," said Judge Hawthorn.

"Yes, Judge, thank you." Brian handed the phone to Mrs. Parrish.

Mrs. Parrish took the phone and said hello.

"Mrs. Parrish, this is Judge Malcolm Hawthorn. I am friends with the Governor of Kansas. I do not want to bother him with this matter, but I will if you do not grant Gary Sands and his wife temporary foster care status and let them take care of the baby they are asking for. There are many children in this country in need of help. You do not turn anyone away who is willing to ease their suffering. So, what will it be, Mrs. Parrish? Do I need to call the governor?"

"No, Judge Hawthorn. I will see that Officer Sands and his wife are granted temporary custody of the child," said Mrs. Parrish.

Mrs. Parrish handed Brian his phone and looked at the assembled group. "It seems, Officer Sands, you will have temporary custody of the child. Will you take him by the clinic and have him checked out. We have to make sure he is okay," she said.

"Yes, I'll call my wife and have her meet me there," said Gary.

"If you have any problems please call my office," she added.

Mrs. Parrish turned and left.

"Thank you," said Gary to Brian. "I had no idea who to call for help."

"It is always important to have someone with pull in your corner," agreed Brian.

Marsha came back in from the front. She looked at Gary and smiled. Sam was sleeping soundly on Gary's shoulder.

"If you need any help just call us. I still have Cindy's baby clothes and blankets. I will round up what I think you can use and bring them over later," she said.

"Thanks," said Gary. "It has been a while since we have needed baby clothes. I am sure Mary will be glad of the help. Would you happen to know where I could get a child car seat?"

"I have one in the trunk of my car. You can use it," said Marsha.

"Thanks," said Gary. He went over to the side and called Mary. He explained the situation to her and asked her to meet him at the clinic. Mary did not ask a bunch of questions. She said she would meet him there. Gary hung up the phone and sighed. He was one very lucky man. He was with the love of his life, and she would be by his side through anything.

Gary went outside to find the car seat ready; he eased Sam into the seat, without waking him, and tucked his blanket in with him. He bade his friends goodbye and drove out of the parking lot on his way to meet Mary.

Mary met him at the clinic. They checked Sam over, without waking him, and pronounced him in good health. They said he was dehydrated and in need of feeding and cleaning up, otherwise he was okay.

Gary and Mary gave a sigh of relief. They paid the bill and

left. Gary put Sam into the car seat in his car, and Mary followed him home. When they entered the house, Laura, Mac, Tilly and Macy were all in the living room. When they saw Sam in Gary's arms, Tilly and Mac started asking questions.

Gary held up his hand for quiet. They hushed and Gary handed Tilly Sam's blanket.

"Would you see this washed so when Sam wakes up, he can have it?" he asked.

"Sure, Dad," said Tilly. She took the blanket and headed for the laundry room.

"I'll take Sam," said Mary. He has got to have a wash. He is sleeping so soundly, maybe I can clean him up without waking him."

Gary surrendered Sam to Mary, but went along with her to help.

"What's going on?" asked Laura.

"Dad and Mom just came in with a baby," said Mac.

"A baby!" exclaimed Laura.

"Well, he looks like he may be a couple of years old," said Macy.

"I wonder where they got him," said Laura.

"He probably needed help, and they volunteered," said Mac.

"Yeah, probably," agreed Laura.

There was a knock at the door. Mac went to answer it. He came back with Brian, followed by Marsha with Cindy in her arms. She also had a bag with diapers in it. Brian was carrying a fold up crib. As soon as he set it down, he headed back to the car to bring in the baby stuff Marsha decided would be needed. Mac went with him to help.

Marsha sat on the sofa next to Laura.

"Do you know what's going on?" asked Laura.

"Lany found the little boy in the alley behind Danny's. We

don't know how he got there, but we are looking into it. Gary and Mary became his temporary foster parents to keep him from being put into a group home," said Marsha. "Once a child is put into a group home, it can take a long time to get them out."

"It's good Mom and Dad could help," said Laura.

"Yeah, it will be nice having a baby around," said Mac.

"I'll remember to call on you for feeding," Gary said to Mac with a grin, as he came into the room and heard Mac's remark.

"Was the baby alright?" asked Marsha.

"Yes, he is fine. A few days of rest and feeding and he will be good as new," said Gary.

Mary entered with Sam in her arms. She saw all the baby things Marsha and Brian had brought over. She turned to them with a smile.

"Thank you so much. I had not even thought of diapers, yet. You can see how long it has been since I have had to care for a baby," she said.

"You are welcome," said Marsha. "They are girl clothes, but as young as he is, he won't care."

Brian and Gary took the folding crib and set it up to one side by the window. Mary took the diapers and, taking the towel from around Sam; put him into a diaper and a tee shirt. When they had the crib ready, she lowered him into it, gently. He curled to one side and slept on. Mary gently covered him with a clean blanket.

They stood watching him sleep for a few minutes.

"I just don't understand how anyone could treat their child like this," said Gary.

Brian clapped him on his shoulder. "Some people have no feelings for anyone but themselves." he said.

"Drugs and alcohol turn decent people into the dregs of society," agreed Marsha.

"I'm glad Lany found Sam before anything happened to him," said Mary.

Gary put his arm around Mary's shoulder and squeezed it tightly.

"Me, too, thanks for going along with the foster care. I did not get a chance to ask you about it first," said Gary.

Mary looked at him in surprise. "Gary Sands, I would have been very upset with you if you had not offered to take care of Sam," said Mary.

Everyone laughed and Gary turned and kissed Mary.

"Heaven forbid you being upset with me," he replied with a smile.

They all laughed again and Brian and Marsha took their leave.

Tilly excused herself to go and retrieve Sam's blanket. She brought it back and laid it in the crib beside him. It was a lovely shade of misty green.

"It's a pretty color," said Mary. "I couldn't tell before. Thanks for washing it, Tilly."

Tilly just smiled at her and went to join Macy on her way upstairs to Tilly's room.

"Are you going to let him sleep down here?" asked Mac.

"No, I'll take the crib upstairs when we go up. I don't want him to wake up alone and be scared," said Gary.

"When he wakes up, I will feed him," said Mary. "I know he has to be hungry. Marsha brought him a couple of sippy cups and a couple of boxes of cereal. I did not want to wake him until he was ready. He will have to have small meals at first. We don't know how long it has been since he has been fed."

"Lany gave him a glass of milk and a few fries, but I am sure he is still hungry," said Gary.

"You are absolutely great parents and great people," said Laura.

"I don't know many people who would step up and help the way you do. I am so proud to be your daughter."

Mary came over and gave her a hug. "I am proud to have you for a daughter," she said.

Gary came over and hugged her, also.

"We are proud of all of our kids," he said. "We have been blessed with a great family. If we can help others along the way, we will always do our best."

Marsha's phone rang while they were on their way home.

"Hello, Sgt. Dane," she answered.

"Sgt. Dane, we have a hit on the baby. It was reported missing day before yesterday in Mountain Springs. His father reported him missing. It seems his mother took him. The father is Officer Samuel Marc Lawson and the baby is Samuel Marc Lawson II. The father and mother are divorced, and the father has custody. The mother slipped him out of daycare and took off with him. We sent out an alert to let the father know his son is alright and gave them your phone number, so you will probably be hearing from him soon."

"Thanks for letting me know," said Marsha, hanging up.

She looked at Brian, who had been sitting patiently, waiting.

"They found Sam's father. His mother kidnapped him day before yesterday. The father has custody. They are divorced. If she makes a habit of leaving little Sam alone, I am not surprised. The station gave them my number, so I'll be hearing from the father, soon."

"Let's get Cindy inside before he calls," said Brian.

They got out and went inside. Marsha fed, bathed, and put Cindy to bed. She had just gotten Cindy to sleep, when the call came from Officer Samuel Lawson.

"This is Sgt. Marsha Dane," answered Marsha.

"Sgt. Dane, this is Officer Samuel Lawson. I understand you found my son."

"He was found in the alley behind Danny's Bar and Grill," said Marsha.

There was a pause, Marsha heard someone cursing. "Is he alright?" asked Samuel.

"Yes, he has been checked out; and apart from being dirty, hungry, and scared, he is fine. He's being taken care of by one of our officers and his wife. He seemed to be more comfortable with someone in uniform," said Marsha.

"I'll be on my way to get him as soon as I hang up," said Samuel.

"He's sleeping now. Morning is soon enough. He is perfectly safe. Bring your custody papers with you when you come," said Marsha.

"Yes, I will. If you see my ex-wife or her boyfriend around, I want them both arrested for kidnapping and child endangerment," said Samuel.

"What is your former wife's name and the name of her boyfriend?" asked Marsha.

"Her name is Beth Grayson and her boyfriend goes by the name of Mule. I don't know his real name. Beth had been denied visitation with Sam when she showed up for a visit high on drugs. I had told them at the daycare she was not to be allowed around Sam, but it seems there was a new employee. Beth made her feel sorry for her and, when the employee turned her back, Beth slipped out with Sam. Believe me, that employee is not at the daycare any longer.

"Do you need directions to Sharpville?" asked Marsha.

"No, I have already looked it up. I'll see you in the morning at the police station," said Samuel.

"Good night," said Marsha.

"It will be a lot better than last night," agreed Samuel'

They both hung up and Marsha turned to Brian. "He will be here in the morning. I had better call Gary and let him know." said Marsha. Marsha turned and called Gary.

"Hello," said Gary.

"Hi, Gary, we got a hit on Sam. His father is a police officer in Mountain Springs. His name is Samuel Lawson. He and his wife are divorced and the father has custody. The mother and her boyfriend kidnapped Sam from his daycare the day before yesterday. The father will be in Sharpville tomorrow. He will be coming to the police station with proof of his right to custody."

"Do I need to bring Sam to work with me?" asked Gary.

"No, let Mary take him to the Little Tots with her. We need to check everything out before we hand Sam over to his father," said Marsha.

"Okay," agreed Gary. "I'll see you in the morning."

Gary turned from the phone and filled Mary in on what Marsha told him. Mary went into his arms and hugged him close. Sam had not been around long, but they were going to miss the little guy. Gary hugged her back with a sigh.

CHAPTER 13

arsha had barely gotten settled in her office the next morning when Officer Samuel Lawson was shown in. Marsha went to meet him and shook his hand.

"It's nice to meet you, Officer Lawson," she said.

"It's nice to meet you. I can't tell you how glad I was to get the report from you guys yesterday. I have been going out of my mind ever since Beth took Sam," said Officer Lawson.

"It sounds like you have a real mess on your hands with her, Officer Lawson," said Marsha.

"Yes," agreed Samuel. "Please, call me Samuel. Beth and I have been divorced since before Sam was born. I caught her with our neighbor. I wasn't even sure Sam was mine until he was born and I had a DNA test done. As soon as I knew for sure he was mine, I filed for custody."

"Do you have the papers with you?" asked Marsha.

"Yes, they are right here," Samuel took the papers out of a brief case and handed them to Marsha.

Marsha looked them over and handed them back to Samuel. "They seem to be in order," said Marsha. "We are going to have to ask you to stay in Sharpville for a couple of days while we check things out and try to catch Beth and her friend."

"Is that really necessary?" asked Samuel.

"Yes, it is. If you leave and take Sam with you, Beth may just follow you and make another try for Sam. If you are here, we can try to catch her in the act," said Marsha.

"Okay, I'll check into the bed and breakfast. My boss gave me a week off to get things settled," said Samuel. "When can I get Sam?"

"I'll take you over to see him, now," said Marsha rising. "I'm going to suggest you leave him in daycare for today while you get a room and get settled. He will be perfectly safe there. He is with Mary Sands. Mary and her husband, Gary, took care of him last night."

Marsha spotted Gary as she left her office.

"Hey, Gary, do you have a minute?" she called. Gary turned and headed for Marsha.

"Gary, this is Officer Samuel Lawson. He is Sam's father."

Samuel reached to shake Gary's hand. "I can't thank you enough for looking after my little boy," said Samuel.

Gary shook his hand. "He is a great little boy. My wife and I enjoyed having a baby in the house once more," said Gary.

"We are headed over to Little Tots," said Marsha.

"I can take him over if you want," said Gary.

"No, I'll go," said Marsha. "It will give me a chance to surprise Cindy with a hug." Marsha smiled and led the way out.

"We'll go in my car," said Marsha when Samuel headed for his car.

Samuel turned and settled himself in the passenger seat of Marsha's car.

When they went into Little Tots, there was a girl sitting on the floor playing with Sam and Cindy. When Cindy saw Marsha, she got up and hurried over to greet her. The girl sitting with them looked around at Marsha and smiled. She looked up at Samuel and froze.

"I'm not ready to go home yet," said Cindy. "I want to play with Sam."

"I'm not here to take you home. I'm here to bring Sam's dad to see him."

Samuel laughed. He had been gazing at Sam with his heart in his eyes. When Sam heard him laugh, he looked around. When he saw his dad, he got up and ran to him as fast as his little legs would let him. Samuel got down on one knee and opened his arms. Sam plowed right into them and put his little arms around his dad's neck and squeezed tightly.

"Hello, Sam, I'm so glad to see you. I missed you a lot," said Samuel.

Samuel leaned back and looked into Sam's face.

"Are you okay?" he asked.

Sam squeezed tighter. "Are you having fun with Cindy?" asked Samuel.

Sam eased up and nodded his head, after a glance at Cindy.

The girl who had been playing with Cindy and Sam came over to them. She stood staring at Samuel. She had not said a word.

Samuel looked up at her noticing her for the first time. He did a double take.

"You are the girl from the mirror," he said. "I thought I was seeing a ghost."

"I'm not a ghost and I did see you in the mirror," she said.

"You saw Samuel in the magic mirror, Crystal?" asked Marsha.

"Yes, I did," agreed Crystal.

"Oh, my," said Marsha with a smile.

"What's a magic mirror?" asked Samuel.

"It's a mirror on display at Danny's. If a girl looks into it, sometimes, it will show them their true love," explained Marsha.

Samuel looked at Crystal and then Marsha. "You don't really believe in such, do you?" asked Samuel.

"Absolutely," said Marsha. "When my husband was missing and presumed dead, the mirror showed him to me. When I knew he was alive, I came to find him. The mirror really works."

Samuel shook his head. He did not want to argue, but he was far from believing in magic mirrors. "I'm sorry Miss, but I just don't believe in magic," said Samuel.

Crystal smiled sadly. She leaned over and patted Sam on his back.

"How can you say that, Samuel, when you are holding the greatest magic of all?" she asked.

"Yes, he is all of the magic in the world," agreed Samuel.

He put his hand over Crystal's to pat it, but pulled back quickly when they both experienced a large shock.

"I'm sorry," said Samuel, looking at his hand curiously.

Marsha turned slightly to hide her big smile. Cindy tugged on her hand,

"I want Sam to come and play with me," she said.

"Do you want to go and play with Cindy?" Samuel asked Sam.

Sam nodded his head and when Samuel put him down, he went back over to the toys they had been playing with before and sat down. Cindy sat down beside him and they started playing. Sam laughed at Cindy, and Cindy laughed back at him.

Samuel relaxed a little when he heard Sam laugh.

"Children bounce back quickly," said Marsha. "Now, we

just have to make sure he stays safe. We need to make sure his mother can't run off with him again."

Crystal had gone back over to the children. She was ignoring Samuel. Samuel looked at her curiously. He did not understand why he was drawn to her and what was with the shock. He shook his head. He would think about all of this later. He had to get a room for him and Sam.

Samuel went over to Sam and knelt down.

"I'll be back in a little while. I'm going to find us a place to stay. You stay here and play with Cindy, okay?" he asked.

Sam looked at him for a minute, then, he nodded and went back to playing. Samuel rose and nodded to Crystal. He went to join Marsha for the trip back to the police station.

Instead of taking him to the police station, Marsha took him to the bed and breakfast. She had stayed there, briefly, when she had first come to Sharpville. She parked the car and they both got out and went in.

"Hello, Marsha," said Mrs. Douglas. "How are you doing? I heard there was going to be another little one."

Marsha laughed. "News sure travels fast in this town," she said. "Mrs. Douglas, this is our friend, Officer Samuel Lawson. He needs a room for a few days and he has a two-year-old so he will need a crib."

Mrs. Douglas turned the book around for him to sign.

"Give me a little while to get Barry to set up the crib and he will be all set," said Mrs. Douglas.

"Great," said Marsha. "Send the bill to Monica at the police station."

"You don't have to do that," said Samuel.

"Monica is in charge of our fund to help families of police officers. This is part of what the fund is for," said Marsha. "We are asking you to stay over."

'Okay," agreed Samuel.

They said good bye to Mrs. Douglas after collecting a key for the room and left. Instead of taking him to the police station, Marsha took him by Danny's. She wanted to show him where Sam had been found, and she wanted to show him the magic mirror.

Brian spotted them as they came in the door. He had already talked to Gary, so he knew who was with Marsha.

"Hi, Beautiful," said Brian, coming over for a kiss.

"Hi, you just made my day," said Marsha with a smile.

"This is Sam's dad, Officer Samuel Lawson," said Marsha. "Samuel this is the love of my life, my husband, Brian Dane."

Samuel grinned. "You are a lucky man, Mr. Dane," said Samuel.

"I know," said Brian. "Call me Brian."

"I'm Samuel," agreed Samuel.

"Sam was found out back," said Marsha. "First, I want to show you the magic mirror."

"Why do you want to show him the magic mirror?" wondered Brian.

"Because, he and Crystal saw each other when Crystal looked in the magic mirror," said Marsha.

"Oh," said Brian.

"You believe a mirror is magic," Samuel said to Brian.

"I know it is," grinned Brian. "It brought Marsha to me when I suffered memory loss. If not for the mirror we would not be together and I might still be without my memory."

"Okay," said Samuel, following Marsha over to the table holding the mirror.

He stood looking at it and reading what it said.

"It won't work for you. It only works for girls looking in it," said Marsha.

She gave him another minute to look at the mirror before she took him through the kitchen and introduced him to Danny and Lany. They then went out into the alley and she showed him where Sam had been found.

"Anything could have happened to him," said Samuel. "We have to make sure he is not in a situation like this again."

Marsha patted his arm. Lany and Brian had followed them out into the alley. "I hope you find the person who left the little fellow here in the alley. He was so scared," said Lany. "They need to be left to fend for themselves in a cold dark place."

"I agree," said Samuel. "Thanks for finding and taking care of him."

"You are welcome," said Lany. He turned and went back inside.

"I have to take Samuel back to his car at the police station," said Marsha to Brian. "I'll see you later." She leaned close for a kiss.

"It was nice meeting you, Brian," said Samuel.

"It was nice meeting you and Sam," said Brian.

They all went back through the building, and Marsha and Samuel went on out to the car, where Marsha, finally, took him to the station to get his car. They said goodbye, and Marsha went inside to let Monica know to expect the bill from the bed and breakfast.

Samuel drove around Sharpville. He wanted to get a feel for the town. He was impressed. It was a small town, but it had everything any town would need for its community. The town was larger than Mountain Springs and had more of a variety of stores. It had a nice sized school and several churches. It looked like a nice town to live in. If the people he met were an example of the community, he was interested.

His parents had retired and moved to Florida. His older brother sold his house and followed them. He wanted his kids to be close to their grandparents. His other brother was in the Navy and hadn't been home in a long time. He and Sam no longer had any family in Mountain Springs. The only family there was Beth's family, and he did not trust them to put Sam's needs ahead of what Beth wanted. He would like to get away from them.

Samuel decided to go by the day care and check on Sam. He wanted to reassure Sam and himself. He was still reeling from finding Sam missing. It would take a while for him to get over the feeling of terror he had felt when he received the news.

Samuel went in the door. Mary was sitting in a rocking chair close to the door. She was feeding a bottle to a small child. She smiled at Samuel and motioned to where Sam and Cindy had joined a group of children gathered around Crystal. Crystal was reading them a story, and they were all watching her and looking at the pictures she was showing with the story.

Sam looked over and spotted his dad. He gave his dad a really big smile, but he stayed beside Cindy in the group and listened to the story. Samuel knew he made the right choice to stop at the day care when he saw the relief on Sam's face at the sight of his dad.

"Did you get set up in a room?" asked Mary.

"Yes, Marsha took me by the bed and breakfast. They are getting a crib set up for Sam," said Samuel.

"Good," said Mary. "You can have the baby supplies we have. Marsha and Brian brought some things over last night. There are some shirts and shorts, diapers, blankets, and some other odds and ends all babies need."

"Thank you, I was in such a hurry to get to Sam, I didn't pack much," said Samuel. "I drove around and looked the town over. You have a nice town. It is larger than Mountain Springs. There seemed to be a nice school. It looked fairly new."

"Yes, we raised money to help build it about five years ago. Marsha had just found Brian and moved here. She told us we had to have decent school. She said no child of hers was going to a tumble-down school and they were not going away to school either." Mary laughed. "When Marsha makes up her mind, she is a force to be reckoned with."

"It sounds like it," agreed Samuel with a laugh.

Mary finished feeding and burping the baby she was holding. She got up to go and lay him down. "You are welcome to sit here and watch Sam as long as you want. I know how nervous you must be to let him out of your sight. I'm glad you are letting him participate with the other children. It will go a long way toward relieving him of the trauma he went through."

"Thank you," said Samuel.

Mary put the baby she was holding in a crib. She rubbed his back until he settled to sleep. She then went and got another bottle. She picked up another baby and headed back to the rocker.

Samuel watched her for a moment.

"Do you have many more to feed?" he asked.

"Just two more left," replied Mary.

"Why don't you let me feed this one and you can get another. You'll get it done faster," said Samuel.

"Are you sure?" asked Mary.

"I've fed many a bottle. I promise I know how it's done," encouraged Samuel.

Mary smiled. She got up and placed the baby in Samuel's arms. She placed a cloth over his shoulder and went to pick up another baby to feed.

Samuel smiled at the little face. Its eyes were staring at him intently. It seemed to be fascinated by a new face. As soon as the milk was gone, Samuel raised the baby to his shoulder and patted its back. He was soon rewarded with a large burp. Mary laughed.

She motioned for Crystal, who was finished with

storytelling, to come and put the baby in its crib. Crystal came over and smiled at Samuel.

"I'll take her now," she said. She reached for the baby and in doing so, her and Samuel's hands met. They both experienced a shock. Crystal had been expecting it this time and continued to take the baby. Samuel looked on in astonishment. He did not understand. He had never been this drawn to another person, not even Sam's mother. He was not sure he knew what to make of it.

Crystal just smiled and went on. Let him figure it out, she thought. The magic mirror said he was meant for her. The magic mirror was never wrong. He would just have to get used to it.

CHAPTER 14

*S*amuel hung around for a couple of hours. He made himself useful and kept an eye on Sam. When he noticed Sam beginning to yawn and look tired, he told Crystal he was taking him to the bed and breakfast, so he could rest.

Crystal smiled and hugged Sam goodbye. Sam turned and kissed her on her cheek. He had noticed other kids doing it when they left. Crystal smiled at him and gave him another hug.

Samuel was surprised to see Sam be so affectionate with anyone. He was usually shy around strangers. Samuel nodded goodbye to Crystal. He did not want to touch her and get shocked again.

After Samuel left, Mary called Marsha. She told Marsha about Samuel being impressed with their town. She was wondering if maybe they could lure him into moving to Sharpville.

"You may have come up with a great idea. Let me do a little checking. I'll let you know what I find out," said Marsha.

Marsha called the Mountain Springs Police Department.

She managed to get a chatty person on the line and soon learned everything she could possibly want to know about Officer Samuel Lawson and his troubles with his ex-wife. She learned about his family moving to Florida. She was also informed that Officer Lawson was a fine police officer.

Marsha hung up with a sigh of satisfaction. She left her office and paid a visit to the chief. She explained about Officer Lawson and received permission to offer him employment at the Sharpville Police Department. Marsha smiled. Now all she had to do was convince Samuel he wanted to move to Sharpville.

Marsha called Marian Embers at her real estate office.

"Hi, Marian, this is Marsha Dane. How are you doing?" asked Marsha. She knew Marian from church and through Marissa. Marian had also helped her and Brian buy the house they were living in.

"We are all doing okay. How about you? I heard about the baby, congratulations," said Marian.

"Thank you, we are very happy. Cindy will make a great big sister," said Marsha.

"What can I help you with today?" asked Marian.

"I have a friend who may need a small house to rent or rent to buy. I was wondering if you have anything like that available."

"As a matter of fact, I just listed a small house today. It is in town and in a nice neighborhood. It can be either rented or rent to own. It is listed at a very reasonable price. It's on Park Avenue, close to the park and children's playground," said Marian.

"It sounds perfect," said Marsha. "Could you put a hold on it for a couple of days while I talk to my friend and get back to you?"

"Okay, but let me know as soon as you can," agreed Marian.

"I will," promised Marsha.

Marsha smiled. Everything was coming together nicely, she thought. After all, Crystal and Samuel deserved a chance to be together. The mirror would not have matched them otherwise.

When Samuel arrived at the bed and breakfast, Mrs. Douglas insisted Sam needed food before going to sleep. She had Samuel bring him into the dining room and proceeded to set plates of food before both of them. When they had finished those plates, she brought each of them a slice of chocolate cake.

"Mrs. Douglas, you are going to spoil us. I have never had cake this good," declared Samuel.

"It's nice to have a little one around to spoil. My grandkids are too far away for me to spoil. I only get to see them once a year. They hardly know me," said Mrs. Douglas sadly.

"I'm sorry," said Samuel. "My folks retired to Florida. Sam doesn't even know them. I hate to see him missing out. Having you to spoil him will be like having an honorary grandmother."

"I'd like that," said Mrs. Douglas with a big smile.

"Well, I had better get this one up for a nap before he falls asleep in his cake," said Samuel with a laugh. "Thanks for the food."

"You're very welcome," said Mrs. Douglas. "If you need anything, just let me know."

Samuel carried Sam up to their room and Mrs. Douglas busied herself clearing the table.

After Mary arrived home from work, she had Mac help her gather the baby supplies Marsha and Brian had brought over. They then took them over to the bed and breakfast for Samuel to use.

Sam was just getting up from his nap when they arrived, and he was ecstatic to receive his baby blanket. He grabbed onto it and rubbed his face in it. Samuel laughed.

"He has always loved his blanket. I wondered where it had gotten to," he said.

"He had it with him when he was found. We washed it before we let him use it. It was filthy," said Mary.

"I want to thank all of you for all you have done for Sam and for me. It has been a while since I have felt so good about being around friends," said Samuel.

"I am glad you consider us friends," said Mary. "It has been a joy taking care of Sam. You should bring him by the day care tomorrow. He would enjoy playing with Cindy and the other youngsters, and he and Crystal really hit it off."

"I'll see. I don't know how long I'll be here. Marsha just said a few days," said Samuel.

"You should think about moving here," said Mary. "It's a great town to live in. People look out for and help each other. I know you could get a job with the police force. We would love to have you and Sam in our community."

Samuel looked surprised. "I have been thinking about looking for more information about what I would need to make the move," said Samuel.

"Good," said Mary smiling. "If you need anything just give us a call." She and Mac left after giving their phone number to Samuel and giving Sam a hug.

Marsha was giving Brian the details of all she did to help Samuel and Sam move to Sharpville. Brian hugged her close and kissed her.

"Don't be too disappointed if he doesn't go along with your plans," said Brian. "Give him room to make up his mind."

"I will," promised Marsha. "I just did not want to give him an excuse to say, no."

Cindy reached up for her daddy to hold her. Brian picked her up and hugged her.

"How is my little Miss?" asked Brian.

"Is Sam going to come and play with me tomorrow?" asked Cindy.

"I don't know," said Brian. "We will just have to wait and see."

Marsha gave Brian a look. Brian shrugged his shoulders and looked resigned. His girls wanted the Lawson family to be added to their friends. He could only hope it all worked out, and they were not disappointed.

The next morning, after eating breakfast and watching a couple of cartoons on television, Sam was getting restless. Samuel looked at him and smiled.

"What is it, Sam? Do you want to go and play with Cindy?" he asked.

Sam jumped up with a big smile and nodded his head vigorously. Samuel laughed.

"Okay, let's go see Cindy and Crystal," said Samuel. Samuel paused. Where had Crystal's name come from? He must have her on his mind for some reason. He shook his head. No way was he ready to go down the relationship road again.

Samuel gathered up Sam and headed for Little Tots.

When they came in the door, Cindy cheered and made a beeline for Sam. Crystal was standing close to the door. She smiled at Mary who was across the room. Mary smiled at Cindy and watched her grab a hold of Sam's hand and tug him along to play with her. Crystal turned to Samuel.

"I'm glad you decided to bring Sam by. Cindy has been

watching the door all morning. She has become very attached to Sam," she said.

Samuel smiled at her.

"Sam has become fond of her, also. He even rates her above cartoons," he said with a laugh.

"Would you like to stay and watch him?" asked Crystal. "We will even let you help feed the babies, again,"

Samuel laughed. "I would love to help feed the babies. I do want to stay close to Sam for a few days, until he gets over being scared," said Samuel.

"Come with me, I'll get you set up," Crystal took his hand to lead him to the kitchen. There was a distinct shock running through both of them. Crystal did not let go of his hand and the shock faded.

Samuel shook his head and let her lead him to the kitchen. They picked up a couple of bottles of formula and, after testing them, went to pick up two babies.

Samuel picked up the same girl he had fed the day before. She grinned up at him. He smiled back. What a cutie, he thought.

He and Crystal sat in rocking chairs to feed the babies. Crystal looked over at Samuel and grinned. He saw her grin and smiled back.

"I have been taking care of Sam since he was born," he said. "His mother was not into taking care of a baby. Her parents wanted to take him, but they wanted to cut me out of his life. I was not going to let them get away with that."

"Of course not," agreed Crystal. "You have done a wonderful job with him. He is a wonderful little boy."

"Why aren't you married raising your own kids?" asked Samuel.

Crystal looked down. "For the last two years I have been taking care of my mom. She died about six months ago, and I haven't felt like getting into the dating crowd just yet," Crystal explained.

"I'm sorry. I should not be asking you those kinds of questions. I am sorry about your mom, too."

"It's okay," said Crystal. "Time makes everything better."

"After I saw you in the mirror, I decided to leave my future up to fate," Crystal said with a smile. "I didn't really think we would ever meet."

"Life is strange," agreed Samuel.

Samuel and Crystal finished feeding and burping their babies and took them to their cribs. They reached for two more to feed. Sam came over to Samuel and watched him feeding the baby. He smiled at Samuel and gently rubbed a finger on the baby's cheek. He laughed and ran back to play with Cindy.

Marsha came in to check on Cindy. Mary had called her and told her Samuel was there. Cindy ran to her to get a hug and then went back to playing with Sam.

"You look like you are having fun," she told Samuel with a grin.

"Yes, I am," agreed Samuel smiling back at her.

"How would you feel about relocating to Sharpville?" asked Marsha.

Samuel started and looked at her curiously. "I have been thinking about it," he admitted. "Well, I would have to find a job," he said.

"I am authorized to offer you a job with the Sharpville Police Department. You would probably have to ride with another officer until you learn your way around, but then you would get your own car, and I'm sure the pay is higher than Mountain Springs," grinned Marsha.

"Impressive," agreed Samuel. "I would also have to find somewhere to live and someone to look after Sam."

"A friend of mine is a realtor. She has a small house. It has just been listed. It is available for rent or rent to own. She is holding off listing it until you see it. It's in a good neighborhood. It's close to a park and a children's playground. I'm sure you could get Sam into Little Tots. I know you would not want him to go back to the place he was taken from," concluded Marsha.

"Why aren't you running the government?" asked Samuel with a grin. "Have you talked to the Chief in Mountain Springs?"

"No, I thought you would want to take care of him," said Marsha.

"Thanks, I think," said Samuel.

He finished feeding and burping the baby he was holding. He passed the baby to Mary, who was standing listening. Then, he turned to Marsha. "What are we waiting for? Let's get Sam and go see the house," he said.

Marsha grinned at Mary and Crystal, while Samuel went to collect Sam. He had to promise him he would get another chance to play with Cindy before he came along without crying.

Marian met them at the house and showed them around. The owner of the house was still there. She was packing and trying to decide what to take with her. She was moving in with her sister and since her sister had a house full of everything, she was having a hard time deciding what she just couldn't live without.

She greeted Samuel and Sam and showed them around. The house had three bedrooms, but one was small, she had been using it as a sewing room. They decided it would make a great nursery for Sam. After she met Samuel and Sam, she absolutely would not consider anyone else for her house. She told Samuel he could keep what furniture he wanted and they would later decide what to do with the leftovers.

Sam loved the house and Samuel thought it was perfect.

They went back to Marian's office to sign the papers. They could take possession in three days. The owner's sister was picking her up then.

After signing on the house, Samuel went by the station and signed to work for the police station. He received a hearty welcome and found out he would be riding with Gary at first. He was to start in a week. He had to have some time to take care of his old life.

Samuel came out of the chief's office and turned to Marsha. He held out his hand and she shook it.

"Thank you, I am glad you are on my team," he said.

Marsha laughed. "I'm just doing my job, and I'm really glad you and Sam are going to be our new friends and neighbors.'

"Me, too," agreed Samuel.

CHAPTER 15

Marsha went by Danny's to tell Brian about Samuel staying. She went in the door to be greeted by Brian.

"Hello, Beautiful," he said, taking her in his arms and pulling her close.

"Don't look back, but the couple at the table in the corner at the back have been arguing. She called him Mule and he called her Beth," whispered Brian.

Marsha stiffened. "I need to tell Danny to save a pie for me. I am craving it something terrible," said Marsha loud enough to be heard.

She headed for the kitchen. When she went into the kitchen, Danny started to say something to her. She held up her hand for quiet and took out her phone.

"This is Sgt. Marsha Dane. I am at Danny's Bar and Grill. I have two suspects in a kidnapping here now. I need back up and tell them to come in silently."

Marsha hung up the phone and took a deep breath. She looked at Danny and Lany.

"Sorry, guys, little Sam's mother and her boyfriend are out front. Please stay back here until we have them in custody."

She went back out front and moved up close to Brian.

"Danny promised he would save me a pie," she said.

She looked in the mirror over the bar and saw Gary and two other police cars stop out front. When they came inside Marsha drew her gun from her purse and led the way to the table.

"Beth Grayson, you and your friend Mule are under arrest for the kidnapping of Sam Lawson. You are also charged with child endangerment for leaving him abandoned in the alley," said Marsha. "Cuff them and read them their rights."

Marsha motioned for Gary to take over.

Lany came out of the kitchen and came over to the table. "You left the little fellow alone in the dark. He was cold and scared. What kind of a person are you?" he demanded.

"I did not know he was left alone," said Beth. "I was told he would be picked up."

"Who was supposed to pick him up?" asked Marsha.

"Shut up, Bitch," said Mule.

"I will not shut up. You told me you had collected the money for him and turned him over. You did not say anything about leaving him in an alley."

"You sold Sam to someone?" asked Marsha.

Beth realized what she had said and looked scared. "I think I need to talk to an attorney," she said.

'Fine," said Marsha. "Take them down to the station and book them," she told the police officers.

As soon as they were gone, she turned to Gary. "I want you to get a statement from everyone here about these two selling Sam. Make sure they will hold up in court.

Gary went around and got statements from everyone.

Marsha turned to Brian. She went into his arms and he held her tight.

"I feel like being sick. How can people like those two live with themselves?" she whispered. Brian just held her closer. He had no answer.

Meanwhile, Laura and Joe had been talking to each other every day. They were both looking forward to being together, and they were getting impatient. Joe had his interview with the guy from the television station and was waiting to hear from him.

Marissa and Jed were spending as much time together as they could. They were both ready to move forward with their relationship. Jed had been shopping for an engagement ring, and was waiting for the perfect time to ask Marissa to marry him. He had been making plans to build them a house on the farm. They were planning on a family, and he decided a family needed room to grow.

They had found out the date of Joe's graduation. It was only a couple of weeks off and they were planning a trip to see him graduate. They had not told Joe. They wanted to surprise him. Joe only had two more tests to finish up. He was sure he was going to be valedictorian.

The Sands family was getting ready to attend Tilly and Macy's graduation. It was just two days off and Tilly's excitement was high. She was very proud of Stephan. He was the valedictorian of their class.

There was quiet a crowd planning to attend. Mary was taking her camera. She wanted to make sure to get lots of pictures. Marsha and Brian and Cindy were planning on going and Samuel and little Sam were going. Since moving to Sharpville was in progress for them, they had been adopted into the Sands family. The entire family treated Sam like he belonged to them. They were honorary grandparents, aunts and an uncle. Macy's family was attending. She had her mother, father, and little brother. Stephan and George were also expecting family to attend. Mary jokingly said they were going to fill up the audience.

Marissa and Jed were also planning to attend. They had a special dinner planned for afterwards. Jed was extremely nervous about the dinner. He decided it was time to propose to Marissa. He just hoped he was not rushing things. He was sure of their feelings. He wasn't sure Marissa was ready to make it official.

The night had finally arrived. Tilly and Macy put on their caps and gowns. They pinned their caps so they would not fall off. They went out into the hallway and met with Stephan and George. Stephan hugged Tilly, and Tilly told him he was going to do great. He was a little nervous about his speech.

Everyone was seated, and the class marched in and took their seats. The principal and the Lt. Governor made a speech. The salutatorian made a short speech. The principal introduced Stephan.

Stephan was a little nervous to start, but soon relaxed. "Welcome all of our families and friends. We are glad so many of you came to wish our graduating class well. We have accomplished a lot in the last thirteen years. Now, ladies and gentlemen of our graduating class, we soar forth out into the world where we will work to become shining examples and stars to the people around us. We go with purpose and determination to be the best of our generation. Good luck to us all."

Stephan ended his speech to thunderous applause. He took his seat and looked at Tilly, who smiled at him and gave him thumbs up.

The students were called and filed by to receive their diplomas. Afterwards, they mingled with family and friends, getting lots of pats on the back and congratulations.

Brian had made arrangements for a celebration at Danny's. The place was closed for regular customers. Only friends and family were to be allowed and no alcohol was to be served. They all piled into their cars and headed to Danny's, all except Marissa and Jed. They had their own plans.

Jed escorted Marissa into the restaurant, and they were seated at a table close to the back. They ordered and, while they were waiting for their food, Jed took hold of Marissa's hand.

"I wanted to tell you about some of the plans I have made," he said.

"Okay," said Marissa. She was wondering why Jed seemed so nervous.

"I have had plans drawn for a house to be built for us at the farm. It will be close to the homestead, but a separate house. It will be more private." He said. "I know I am doing this all wrong. I want you to be my wife. I want us to live in the new house together and have a family there. Will you marry me and be my love forever?"

"Yes," whispered Marissa with tears in her eyes.

Jed rose from his chair and drew her into his arms. They exchanged a long kiss. When they stopped for air, Jed looked around and smiled at everyone watching them.

"She said, 'yes,'" he said. Everyone started clapping and cheering.

Jed pulled the ring out of his pocket and placed it on Marissa's finger. Marissa held her hand up and admired the ring.

"It's beautiful," she said. She leaned over and they kissed again.

The waitress brought their food. They tried to eat, but were so busy looking into each other's eyes, they were hardly aware of eating.

At Danny's everyone was having a great time. Cindy and Sam were enjoying all of the attention they were receiving. While everyone was busy celebrating, Laura wandered over to the table with the mirror. She had been there so many times with Marissa, she found it easily. She sat down and sighed.

"If only I could get my sight back so I could see Joe graduate," she said.

A white light came from the mirror and bathed Laura in light. It only lasted a few seconds, but everyone stopped and stared. Brian and Marsha rushed over to see about Laura. Mary and Gary were with them.

"Are you alright, Laura?" asked Brian.

Laura looked up at him and smiled.

"I'm fine. I asked the magic mirror to let me see, so it did," Laura smiled again. "I can see."

"It healed you!" exclaimed Mary.

"Yes," agreed Laura. "I can see just fine."

"Well," said Marsha. "The magic mirror is full of surprises."

"Did you know it could do this?" asked Gary.

"No, if I had known I would have had Laura to try it a long time ago," said Marsha.

Mary took Laura in her arms and hugged her tightly. She had tears on her face. Gary put his arms around the two of them and his eyes were wet as he hugged the two of them.

There was many a wet eye in Danny's as everyone realized what had happened. They all huddled around Laura and congratulated her.

Laura looked at Tilly and smiled.

"I'm sorry we are disrupting your celebration," she said.

"Don't be sorry," said Tilly reaching in for a hug. "I am glad it happened now, it put a cap on my celebration. I am so happy for you."

"Thank you," said Laura hugging her back.

"If word gets out about this, there will be a stampede on Danny's. The mirror is going to be more popular than ever," said Marsha.

"Bring it on," said Brian with a smile.

Laura sat down and looked in the mirror. Joe's face looked back at her.

"Joe," she exclaimed. "I can see."

"Wow," exclaimed Joe. "When did it happen?"

"Just now, I asked the mirror to be able to see your graduation and it healed me with a white light," said Laura. "I will be able to see you get your diploma."

"I can't wait. I have some news, too. I heard back from the television station. You are looking at their newest employee," said Joe with a smile.

"Great, I am so glad you are moving back here," she said.

"Me, too, I love you. I can't wait to hold you in my arms," said Joe.

Laura looked around at the crowd around her and then back at Joe.

"I love you, too. I'll see you soon." She said. The mirror

faded back to regular. Laura sighed and then sat up with a smile.

"Joe got the job at the television station. He will be moving back here after graduation," she said.

Everyone agreed this was the best graduation celebration in town.

Jed and Marissa picked up Sara and then came by for Laura. Jed was driving them to Kansas City for Joe's graduation. Marissa made reservations at a bed and breakfast for them. They knew it would take a couple of days rest before they returned to Sharpville. Since Laura told Joe she was going to be at his graduation, they decided not to try to surprise him. Laura told him they were coming, and he was looking forward to seeing Laura.

When she told him his mom was coming, he got all choked up. He missed his family. It would be great to make peace and be part of a family again. Joe knew it was time to put his troubles with Jed behind him. He did not want to start his life with Laura with a feud.

Marissa and Laura were best friends. He knew he and Jed would have a lot of interaction once they were all together. Laura received a miracle with her sight. He was not going to be a downer.

As time got closer for them to arrive, Joe got more and more nervous. He decided to go over to their bed and breakfast and wait for them there. Anything was better than sitting around in his room.

Joe went into the front room of the bed and breakfast and introduced himself. He told the person there he was waiting for his family. He sat on a sofa and picked up a magazine to read.

He really wasn't reading anything. He was just looking at pictures.

He had been waiting for about an hour when he looked up and saw his mom and Laura come in the door. They were followed by Marissa.

Joe hurried over and hugged his mom. He smiled at Marissa and reached out a hand to Laura. Laura took his hand and started at the shock she received. Joe pulled her close into his arms and kissed her soundly.

"It is so good to finally get to hold you in my arms," he whispered.

"Yes," agreed Laura. "I can't believe I can see you."

Joe pulled her closer to him and held her.

Jed coming in with some of their suitcases stopped and stared at Joe. He had not expected Joe to be waiting for them. Joe, seeing Jed, let go of Laura and went over to him. He grinned at Jed.

"Need a little help?" he grinned.

Jed gave a sigh of relief and grinned back.

"Yeah, there are more in the car," he said.

"I'll go and get them. You get signed in," said Joe.

"Okay," agreed Jed.

He put the cases down and went to the desk to sign them in.

Joe brought the rest of their bags in and added them to the pile.

Laura came over and took his hand. They ignored the shock and held on. Joe pulled her close to his side.

"When are you coming to Sharpville?" asked Sara.

"The graduation is tomorrow. I have already turned in my notice, so I thought I would head out the next day," said Joe.

"We are going back then, too," said Marissa. "Maybe we can follow each other."

"You must be Marissa. Hello. It's nice to meet you," said Joe.

Marissa came over and stuck out her hand. Joe took her hand and shook it. "I'm glad to meet you, too," she said.

Joe looked at her ring.

"You and Jed are engaged?" he asked. "Congratulations," he said at her nod.

Jed came over and put his arm around Marissa. "We are all signed in. All we need is to get all of these bags to our rooms."

"You are lucky. Marissa could have decided she needed more shoes," teased Laura.

Jed groaned and Marissa grinned.

"I can't help it. I love shoes," she said.

Jed kissed her on her cheek. "For you I will build a special closet just for shoes. Just keep them there and out of your suitcases."

"I only brought three pairs," protested Marissa.

Jed stared at her, and Laura giggled. Sara gave Marissa a fond look.

"Jed, stop teasing Marissa and get us settled in a room," she said with a smile.

"Okay, Mom," said Jed.

He and Joe grabbed the bags and headed for the rooms. Marissa and Laura were sharing a room. Sara had her own room, and Jed had his own room.

Marissa grabbed her bags and followed Jed into his room. He pulled her close and kissed her.

"Are you sure," he asked.

"Yes, we probably won't be able to get away for a honeymoon. We are here, now and I love you. We are building a life together. It starts now," said Marissa. She was not getting any arguments from Jed. He was ready to start building a life with Marissa.

The rest of them ignored Jed and Marissa. Joe took his mom and Laura out for a meal. They had a very nice time. Joe caught up on all of the hometown news, but he held onto Laura's hand and kept her close to his side.

Joe had his stuff packed and ready to load. After graduation, they went out to eat. Everyone congratulated Joe on being valedictorian of his class. They had a happy time, with Joe teasing Laura about her schoolgirl crush and Jed teasing Marissa about her failed prom date. They all laughed and had a good time. Sara was very relieved to have her boys being civil to each other. They had an early night so they could get an early start back the next day,

Sara and Marissa rode with Jed and Laura rode with Joe. Joe had his car packed with everything he had accumulated while living in Kansas City.

It was a happy group who pulled into Sharpville later in the day. They were ready to start the rest of their lives. With a little help from the magic mirror, they were off to a good start.

ABOUT THE AUTHOR

With five children, ten grandchildren and six great-grandchildren I have a very busy life, but reading and writing have always been a very large and enjoyable part of my life. I have been writing since I was very young. I kept notebooks, with my stories in them private. I didn't share them with anyone. They were all hand-written because I was unable to type. We lived in the country and I had to do most of my writing at night. My days were busy helping with my brothers and sister. I also helped Mom with the garden and canning food for our family. Even though I was tired, I still managed to get my thoughts down on paper at night.

When I married and began raising my family, I continued writing my stories while helping my children through school and into their own lives and families. My sister was the only one to read my stories. She was very encouraging. When my youngest daughter started college, I decided to go to college myself. I had taken my GED at an earlier date and only had to take a class to pass my college entrance tests. I passed with flying colors and even managed to get a partial scholarship. I took computer classes to learn typing. The English language and literature classes helped me to polish my stories.

I found public speaking was not for me. I was much more comfortable with the written word, but researching and writing the speeches was helpful. I could use information to build a story. I still managed to put my own spin on the essays.

I finished college with an associate degree and a 3.4 GPA. I won several awards including President's list, Dean's list, and Faculty list. The school experience helped me gain more confidence in my writing. I want to thank my English teacher in college for giving me more confidence in my writing by telling me that I had a good imagination. She said I told an interesting story. My daughter, who is a very good writer and has books of her own published, convinced me to have some of my stories published. She has them published for me. The first time I held one of my books in my hands and looked at my name on it as author, I was so proud. They were very well received. This was encouragement enough to convince me to continue writing and publishing. I have been building my library of books written by Betty McLain since then. I also wrote and illustrated several children's books.

Being able to type my stories opened up a whole new world for me. Having access to a computer helped me to look up anything I needed to know and expanded my ability to keep writing my books. Joining Facebook and making friends all over the world expanded my outlook considerably. I was able to understand many different lifestyles and incorporate them in my ideas.

I have heard the saying, watch out what you say and don't make the writer mad, you may end up in a book being eliminated. It is true. All of life is there to stimulate your imagination. It is fun to sit and think about how a thought can be changed to develop a story, and to watch the story develop and come alive in your mind. When I get started, the stories almost write themselves, I just have to get all of it down as I think it before it is gone.

I love knowing the stories I have written are being read and enjoyed by others. It is awe inspiring to look at the books and think I wrote that.

I look forward to many more years of putting my stories out there and hope the people reading my books are looking forward to reading them as much.

Love's Sight
ISBN: 978-4-86751-854-0

Published by
Next Chapter
1-60-20 Minami-Otsuka
170-0005 Toshima-Ku, Tokyo
+818035793528

9th July 2021

Lightning Source UK Ltd.
Milton Keynes UK
UKHW010636290721
387974UK00002B/553